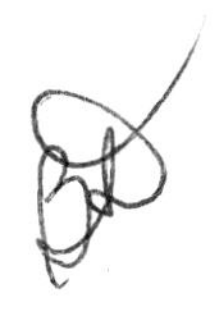

Mystic Murder

A Witches of Hemlock Cove Mystery

By Kennedy Chase

Monty's Tale Press

Copyright

First Published in 2016 by Monty's Tale Press

Chapter One

Just because I have certain abilities doesn't mean finding bodies was something I particularly looked forward to. Being a witch didn't make me any less sensitive or upset about a murder.

The latest one was the most bizarre yet, and the small town of Hemlock Cove was abuzz with rumors as soon as it got out. Things like this never took long to spread like wildfire throughout the New England, coastal town.

It had always been that way, ever since my family, the Angelos, settled there after fleeing the Salem witch trials. They discovered a nice little cove a few miles north of Salem and, along with bootleggers and pilgrims escaping the British colonies, founded Hemlock Cove.

Ever since then, there has been a member of my family present in the town, or more specifically, our old guesthouse on the cliff, imaginatively named The Cliffside Guesthouse.

Our family had a mixed reception here in the Cove, some thought we were evil with our links to Salem, while others saw us for what we actually were: good people who lived to help others in our small, vibrant town.

Our reputation was put into question again when the events of last week began to unfold, dragging my two sisters and me into a world of mystery and murder, but I'm getting ahead of myself. Let me start at the beginning…

I finally blew out the candle in my bedroom around midnight.

It was chilly outside and I could hear the waves of the Atlantic crashing against the cliff. A cool breeze managed to find a way through the old windows, making my breath plume.

"It's going to be a cold one tonight," I said as I pulled the quilt up around my neck and sank into my super-soft down pillow.

My beloved pets snuggled up either side of me on the bed, pinning me in place with their warm, furry little bodies.

On my left lay my gorgeous chocolate Labrador, Noah, and on my right, my fluffy white cat called Charity. She was purring deeply, content with her place by my belly.

Noah was all stretched out on top of the quilt, and I could feel his heat against my leg.

I reached my hands out to pet the animals before getting comfy, ready for a good sleep. I had just finished working a twelve-hour shift in the family bakery located on the ground floor of our old, crumbling guesthouse.

The place wasn't in good enough shape these days to take in guests, so we converted the kitchens and now ran a successful bakery supplying the Cove with all kinds of delicious goods concocted by my older sister, Joy, who was a whizz with herbs and spices.

That was her 'ability'. She could do wonders with the right ingredients.

I didn't get those skills from our parents. Instead, my area of witchcraft expertise was the ability to see things… it's kind of difficult to explain, but you'll see as I continue my tale. Oh, and one small thing that's kind of important: Noah and Charity were named after my parents.

So, I was all tucked in and ready to give my forty-five-year-old bones a good rest when I heard a pair of footsteps outside in the hall.

"Good night, Grace," Joy said from outside of my bedroom door.

"Sweet dreams, Joy," I replied, following our little ritual we repeated every night.

Her footsteps disappeared and her door closed with a creak confirming she had joined her husband, Nathaniel, for the night.

We were a small household, really, considering the size of the house. Other than those I've already mentioned, we were home to just one other member of the Angelo family: Hope.

Hope was our older sister who lived in the top room of

the tower, much to everyone's concern. We knew it wasn't entirely safe up there, especially for Hope, who was now sixty-five.

Nathaniel, bless him, did what he could around the place with repairs and maintenance, but we weren't wealthy and the tower was in such a state of disrepair that all he could do was patch it up.

But Hope never seemed to mind. She would occasionally take visitors but other than that, often kept out of the way, leaving Joy and me to run the bakery.

With my furry bed warmers snoring away, it didn't take me long to drift off to sleep and into a vivid dream. I saw two men, dark shapes mostly, chasing through the woods that surround the Cove. It seemed to me that the man in front was being pursued for some reason.

I woke with a start as Charity leapt on to my chest and batted me on the forehead with her paw.

"Hey," I said, "what's the emergency?"

Mrow! Charity said, her white whiskers barely visible in the predawn light.

Noah yapped from across the room. I looked over to see him standing by the door, wagging his tale. Charity leapt off the bed and joined him so that both were staring at me.

If either of them had opposable thumbs, then they would have opened the door themselves, I'm sure. Noah especially had that look in his eye. The look that transferred some deeper thought process.

"What is it, boy?" I asked.

He woofed quietly and continued to stare at me.

I got out of bed, clutching my pajamas close around my body, grimacing against the chill.

The amulet my mother had left to me was cool against my skin. I reached up for it, as I always did in times of nervousness; it had the effect of keeping me calm and along with my family was my most prized possession. I always slept with it on, not wanting to leave it out anywhere.

Kneeling in front of Noah, we locked eyes and I saw the image of two men being chased again. Only this time, the chaser caught the one in front and a fight broke out.

Charity wound herself around my leg, tickling me with her tail as she flickered it impatiently.

The vision dissipated and Noah tapped the door with his paw.

"Okay, let's see what you two want, but if it's more of my specialty doggy bakes, I won't be happy! They're for Miss Dechamps up in the Ocean View community. She'll have my head if I don't deliver them tomorrow for her precious Chihuahua."

Woof.

Noah didn't seem to care too much about Miss Dechamps.

"Fine," I said, opening the door. "Let's see what the fuss is about."

Charity spun round my leg once before darting out. Noah followed her and I followed them both down the corridor and down the old, creaky staircase until we were in the main parlor of the house.

They led me through to the kitchen and I was about to reach out for Noah to stop him from getting to the tins of doggy bakes I had placed on the counter so I didn't forget to deliver them to Miss Dechamps, when both he and Charity ignored the table of baked goods and ran straight for the large bread oven.

A terrible feeling of dread curled around my stomach, but I stepped further into the dark room, my feet not even noticing the normal coldness of the tiles. My whole body had gone up a few degrees. My witchy intuition was kicking in big time.

I reached out for Noah to pull him away from the oven and was nearly knocked backward with the force of the vision that came to me through him. I could see the trail of scents as if through his eyes.

The kitchen was in a huge mess. Plates and tins lay everywhere, all covered in two distinct scents. If you were to color them somehow, it would look as if a child had gone crazy with a paintbrush and splattered paint all over the floor and walls.

But this wasn't paint or even visible to the naked eye. It was Noah showing me what he could smell, and it looked exactly like a scene of great struggle.

I knew this from experience. Before I joined Joy and Hope in the family bakery business, I was a cop in the tiny Hemlock Cove PD—essentially an outpost of the Salem PD. I retired five years ago when my husband, my police partner at the time, was killed on duty while on transfer to Boston.

Unable to get over that, I left the police, vowing never to get involved again, but these things have a habit of hanging around.

"Charity, come away from there. You too, Noah," I said, shooing them away from the bread oven. Both animals were on edge; their fur prickled. I could feel it from them inside of me, my connection with their spirits an unbroken link.

They did as they were told, and I swung open the large metal door.

I gasped and staggered back. Noah woofed once, twice, and then ran out of the kitchen and up the stairs, presumably to wake the others. Charity let out a sad whine and rubbed up against my leg.

Before me, inside the oven and folded up in a tight ball, was a man.

"Oh my!" I said. "Are you…?" I began to say, but I knew it was too late.

The man was dead.

Dried blood covered the side of his head. He looked as if he'd taken a blow with a bludgeoning weapon.

"What's going on?" a male voice called from the kitchen entrance.

The lights flickered on and Nathaniel stepped inside with Noah right behind him. Nathaniel ran a hand over his short-cropped brown hair and through his neatly trimmed beard before pulling his robe close around his formerly athletic, now slightly softer, body.

"There's a… body in the oven," I said, not quite believing the words myself. But with the strong kitchen lights on, I could see the man more clearly now.

His head had indeed been caved in. I winced looking at him.

Nathaniel came closer and held my elbow with that brotherly gesture of his. "I don't believe it," he whispered as though speaking louder would wake the dead. "That's Gregory Pelt. What on earth is he doing in there, in that state?"

My legs shook and my guts cramped as it fully dawned on me.

Greg Pelt was the owner of the local bar, The Lucky Clover. I hated the thought instantly, but it came nonetheless: he hadn't been very lucky at all given the state he was in now.

"We ought to check for signs of life," Nathaniel said.

"Signs of what?" Joy responded as she came walking into the kitchen, rubbing her eyes and her robe flapping behind her in her haste.

When she looked up and saw poor Greg in the oven, she screamed. And that was my cue to call the police. Given the deathly pallor of Greg's skin, it was quite clear he was dead, and had been for more than a few hours.

I moved over to the doorway where we kept our old corded phone and dialed the local station, knowing it would go through quicker than going via the 911 dispatch. It wasn't like there was an emergency: Greg wasn't going anywhere in a hurry, sadly.

The call was answered on the second ring.

"Police Department," the grizzled voice said. It was a voice that had been shaped by decades of cigars and black coffee and one that I recognized instantly.

"Officer Blackmore… I mean, Logan, it's Grace. There's been an accident," I said.

"Grace? Are you okay? Are you hurt?"

"No, it's not me, it's Gregory Pelt."

"What's happened? Is Greg okay?" Logan said. "There was some trouble at the bar tonight. Some feud between the Kings and the Mannings. Greg had to throw 'em out, did they do something to him?" His voice was now sharp and attentive; the panic in *my* voice clearly communicating to him it was something bad.

Although old and crotchety, Logan Blackmore had always looked out for me when I was on the force and had got to know me well, as I did him. For instance, I knew that he and Greg were best pals, which made it all the more difficult.

"I'm afraid it's terrible news, Logan," I said. "Greg's dead."

Chapter Two

"This is so awful," Joy said. "Poor Greg."

My sister stood beside me as we both watched the two police officers run the crime scene. We were stood in the doorway between the kitchen and the parlor, peering over the yellow police tape.

I knew the two officers from my time in the force, but they didn't talk with me, preferring to focus on their job. They had asked us what we knew, which was nothing.

"Why would anyone want to do this to Greg?" Nathaniel said from behind us. He wrung his hands together as he always did in times of stress.

"I truly don't know," I said. "Logan mentioned something about an argument in the bar tonight between the Kings and the Mannings. Greg apparently had to throw them out."

"You think it could be one of those that did this?" Joy said to me, a look of horror on her face. Joy was ten years older than me at fifty-five, not that she looked it, really. That was one quirk of our family genes: we generally looked much younger than our years.

Of course, there were reasons for that. Reasons that many folk in the town were suspicious about. With our reputation and history of witchcraft, there were all kinds of wacky ideas about. The truth was, Joy was just good with herbs and knew how to use them to help keep our bodies working well and our skin fully hydrated and full of essential vitamins and nutrition.

Some thought that was black magic or some other diabolic effect. It never occurred to them that witchcraft could be used for good, subtle things. We weren't pointy-hat-wearing witches turning people into toads or anything, although sometimes I thought Hope would like that, being stuck up in her tower all day and night.

"When is Detective Jackson due to arrive?" Nathaniel asked.

One of the officers working the crime scene looked over her shoulder at us and said, "Should be any minute. He was already awake when we called him. Now, are you three sure there's nothing else you can tell us about what happened?"

"I'm sorry, Laney," I said. "We've told you everything we know. If it wasn't for Noah and Charity waking me up, I wouldn't have even known he was in there… not until the morning. Well, you can imagine the kind of shock that would be."

"Indeed," Laney said. She turned her attention back to the footprints in the flour, snapping off a number of photographs with the large camera around her neck.

I turned away from the scene and joined Nathaniel on the couch.

Joy sat opposite in her favorite armchair. I poured us three cups of herbal tea and passed them around.

We sat there in silence, drinking our tea, when a few minutes later the doorbell rang.

The sudden chime nearly made me drop the cup. Noah leapt to his feet and padded to the front door, woofing quietly. I stood up and opened it to find Detective Zachary Jackson standing in the doorway, rainwater dripping off his long raincoat.

He was like a vision from a twenties noir story. He

even had the trilby hat that darkened his already dark face. Noah sniffed his hand before licking him.

"Nice to see you again, Zach. It's been a while," I said, and then realized how stupid that sounded given the circumstances. He hadn't come round for tea and cake. I quickly added, "Though I'd prefer it weren't in such a murder-related situation."

"I came as quickly as I could," he said, his voice low and gravelly. "Logan told me right away. The poor guy's in shock."

"I think we all are," Joy said from her armchair. "Well, Grace, let the detective in so he can do his job."

"Oh, of course," I said, stepping back and letting Zach in.

"Detective Jackson," Laney called, "we're in here. We've finished processing the scene and have taken statements. There's little else for us to go on right now. The medical examiner is due soon."

"Thanks, Laney." Zach turned back to face me. He smiled a small, pained smile. We had known each other for nearly twenty years. He was transferred to the Cove's PD when he was just twenty-one.

I had had the honor of training him up before he took his detective training. He was our only detective in the Cove and was effectively on loan from Salem PD, but his bosses had got used to him being out here, and he kind of stayed and had now become a firm fixture of the town.

"So, Grace," he said, "tell me everything that happened, right from the start." He pulled out his notepad and jotted down everything I said, essentially repeating what I had already told the officers, but I knew the procedure and just went with it.

After a few minutes of him questioning me, he moved into the crime scene and spoke with the officers. I was left in the parlor to drink more of Joy's herbal remedy. I had to admit, it was helping, but I couldn't be sure if it really was that or if it was Zach's company.

Despite being a slightly disheveled, tall, wiry figure, he had a dark brooding air to him that I wasn't too modest to admit that I found attractive, though given our age difference, his thirty-nine to my forty-five, I knew it was just a minor crush.

"We're going to need to take this," Zach said, appearing in the doorway. He held a bag containing a rolling pin.

"You think that might be the murder weapon?" Nathaniel asked.

Zach shrugged. "We're going to run it for analysis, but it could be. We'll know more after the autopsy and the tests come back. There's something else," he said. "I'm afraid we're going to have to shut the bakery down for the foreseeable future. We'll have an officer stationed here at the scene in case we need to come back."

"Oh no! This is a disaster," Joy said. "We're supposed to be supplying a full banquet to Mary McDare's Ocean Drive Women's Network function in two days."

"I'm sorry, but I can't have you girls baking in a murder scene."

"What are we going to do?" Joy said. "We really need this contract. If it gets out we couldn't do it, our reputation will be in the gutter!"

"Calm down, dear," Nathaniel said. "I'm sure we'll figure something out. Won't we, Grace?" He looked up at me, full of expectation.

Thanks, I thought. Put all the pressure on me. "I'm sure we'll figure something out, sis," I said, though I had no idea how. While we were trying to come up with some ideas of how we could meet the order for the banquet, Zach came back into the parlor and stood close to me.

His voice low, he said, "Can I talk with you privately?"

I looked up into those deep, soulful eyes of his and nodded. I led him through a door to the right of the parlor that took us into a small library that was my home whenever I wasn't working in the kitchen or taking the animals for a walk.

Charity was already inside, curled up on my favorite chaise. I didn't want to disturb her, so I sat on the edge of my big antique desk. Zach closed the door behind him and stood in front of me. His raincoat hung off his bony shoulders, aiding his wiry shape.

"This really doesn't look good," he said.

"What do you mean? You don't suspect one of us, do you?"

He quickly shook his head. "No, of course not, though

strictly I can't rule anything out, you know that. I have to follow this through properly."

"Yeah, I know. You have to do your job," I said.

He stepped closer and reached out for my elbow. "I promise I'll do this to the letter. Your family will be cleared."

"It won't matter," I said. "You know what this town's like for gossip. Having a dead body turn up in the Angelos' kitchen will only fuel the rumors about our witch heritage and what we can and can't do."

"To hell with them," he said. "In fact, I want you to help me on the case. I want to bring you in as a consultant. I've already cleared it with the DA's office."

"What?" I said, my jaw dropping.

I hadn't worked on a case since I left the force. Occasionally, I had helped Zach out with a few basic questions or just to chat about a case over coffee and cake, but not in an official capacity.

"The way I see it," he said, "you're the best person for this job." He looked over at Charity and then back to me. I knew what he was hinting at: my ability, my affinity with Noah and Charity.

"It's because of the feud, isn't it?" I said. "Between the Kings and the Mannings. If they're involved in this somehow, that's going to be difficult to investigate."

"That's part of it," he said. "Before I came over, I spoke with Janice at the bar. She told me what happened in the bar. Things got real heated. It seems Greg finally had enough of his bar getting smashed up and not so politely asked the two families to leave—with a shotgun."

"He shot them?" I said.

"No, no, nothing like that. He just used it to persuade them to take their fight outside."

"I can't imagine either Callum King or Suzanne

Manning taking too kindly to a threat like that."

Zach shook his head, agreeing. He sat down on the arm of a chair and sighed before looking up at me. "It's a bad one," he said. "The animosity between those two families has been getting worse lately. I fear that Greg got involved at the wrong time and set one of them over the edge."

"Who was involved in the fight at the bar?" I asked.

"Callum, Abe, and David from the Kings, and Suzanne and Matt Manning."

"And do we know what they were fighting over?"

Zach checked his notebook, flicking back through some pages. "Something about a deal that went wrong, but Janice was saying that somehow Greg was involved with one of the King girls."

It didn't come as a huge surprise to me to hear that. Greg Pelt was a known player, working his way through almost every eligible young woman in the Cove. If he had got involved with one of the King girls, then I could see how that would make things difficult for him. Callum, the old patriarch of that family, was both headstrong and bad tempered.

There were more than a few boys in the Cove who had made the mistake of getting with one of Callum's granddaughters or nieces.

"Surely, even Greg wouldn't be stupid enough to go there?" I said.

"Who knows? This is why I want you to work on this with me. I'm going to need someone who can get information without making either family defensive. You know what they're like: they'll clam up and circle the wagons as soon as I start the investigation. So, will you consult with me on this, Grace, like the old days?"

Before I had a chance to answer, the door opened.

Laney poked her head through. “The medical examiner is here, boss.”

“Thanks, I'll be right there.”

Laney nodded once and closed the door behind her.

“I should go,” Zach said and reached out, touching my arm. “Think about it. Meet me at the Bean and Broomstick tomorrow noon and we can talk more about it. I should have more information by then.”

And that was that.

He left me there wondering what I had let myself in for. I knew in that instant that I would work with Zach. And somehow help Joy find a way of meeting the banquet order.

Charity opened one eye and flicked her tail at me.

“I know,” I said. “I wouldn't have been able to stop you or Noah from investigating even if I tried. Just don't get me into trouble, okay?”

Charity *merped* once and closed her eyes again.

Trouble was her specialty, and I knew I was in for a lot of it.

Chapter Three

I woke early the next day at 06:30. Laney had stayed in one of our least-wrecked guest rooms overnight as per the law; she needed to stay on the site of the crime scene if Zach wanted to come back to it later.

That was one of those things they often got wrong in shows like *CSI* or *Law & Order*.

Even though I loved watching them, it did annoy me that they got basic things wrong like having detectives return to the scene of crime for more evidence.

That kind of evidence wasn't permissible in court. Once the scene had been left, it was all too easy for it to get contaminated. Laney staying on site in a shift pattern with her partner meant that the scene was active for investigation until they left.

Of course, the major downside to having our kitchen regarded as an active crime scene was the lack of access to the coffee machine and waffle maker. We weren't allowed to touch a thing.

Laney was sitting in the parlor, filling out paperwork on our antique coffee table when I entered with Noah and Charity stuck to my legs like glue.

"They absolutely love you, don't they, Grace?" Laney said, pointing her pen at my pets.

"They sure do. It has its benefits."

"I'm sure it does." Laney looked at me with a knowing

smile.

She knew the rumors, as did everyone else in the town. Given that Charity would often walk with me into town, I was often referred to as the 'Crazy Cat Witch of Hemlock Cove'.

I didn't mind the cat witch part, as that wasn't too far from the truth, but I wasn't in the least bit crazy. That attribute was our elder sister Hope's specialty.

As far as I was concerned, I was completely sane… well, almost completely.

“Oh, Grace, I hope you don't mind, I ordered coffee and croissants in from the Bean and Broomstick. I felt bad about you guys not being able to use your kitchen. It'll come off expenses.” The young officer gestured to a brown bag, in which were half a dozen coffee cups and croissants.

“They smell delicious! Thanks, that's very kind of you.”

I sat down and sipped the coffee. Charity hopped up onto the coffee table and padded across Laney's paperwork, purring and merping as she brushed her tail across the officer's face.

"Hey," Laney said, "how am I supposed to get any work done with you being all cute, huh?"

After a few circuits across the papers, Charity slumped down on the table and curled up. Noah was sat at my feet, with his chin on his paws. I sat back and let the coffee enter my system. It helped take away some of the anxiety over the whole situation with Greg.

"So, how's it going, with the crime scene, Laney? Found anything useful?"

Laney pulled a strained expression. "I'm sorry, I can't really tell you that. It'll all be going in a report to Zach, so I'll have to leave that up to him what he's willing to share."

"That's fair enough," I said. I wanted to pull the 'I'm a consultant' card, but I knew she was just doing her job, so I left it.

I nibbled on a croissant in silence as she continued to work on her report, all the while trying to rack my brains as to what we were going to do for this networking event of Mary McDare's.

I didn't have long to think when I heard Joy's excited voice coming down the stairs and into the parlor. Nathaniel was close behind her. "I don't know what we're going to do!" Joy said for the third time. "It's a disaster. We're going to be ruined!"

Out of the three of us, Joy looked the most like our mother: big white-blonde curly hair, blue eyes, and a curvy body that spoke of cuddles.

Joy was ten years my senior and was the glue between me and Hope, who at sixty-five was more like a matriarchal figure to me than a sister.

"Morning, Grace," Nathaniel said, trying to lift the mood. "Did you sleep okay?"

"Not too bad," I said. "You don't look like you fared too well, though."

He really didn't. His usual bright green eyes and smile had disappeared to be replaced with a dull, tired expression. His eyes were rimmed with red and his normally neat beard looked spikier as though he had experienced a rough night.

"It wasn't easy," he said. "I couldn't get the image of Greg out of my mind."

"I offered to make him something," Joy said, "but he would have none of it."

Joy was, of course, referring to one of her specialty herbal remedies. She has this particularly interesting recipe that can help remove memories for a while—and the reverse: restore them. She didn't often make use of them, though. We all tried to keep a low profile in the Cove, not wanting to add any more fuel to our reputation.

"Mr. and Mrs. Angelo," Laney said, standing up, "I'm really sorry for all the inconvenience. Here, I've bought you breakfast. I'll continue to work in the kitchen and give you guys some space."

"You're a darling, Laney," Joy said, giving the young officer a tight hug, surprising her. Joy was always like that: super tactile. It suited her name, really. "Thank you for the kind thought."

Laney smiled and slinked off into the kitchen to leave us alone in the parlor.

"She called again this morning," Joy said. "Can you believe it? At this time of morning too."

"Who?" I asked.

"McDare. About that blasted banquet. She wants to taste samples tomorrow afternoon. You know me, Grace, I'm a patient woman, but McDare… she's pushing me to my limits. She even said she heard about Greg and hinted that somehow it was our fault for not having better security."

"That'll be all round the Cove by now, then," Nathaniel said. "That woman has connections up the wazoo."

"Do you want me to speak with her?" I said, regretting it even as the words came out of my mouth.

"Thank you, but it's best if I deal with it," Joy said. "Besides, you'll be seeing Miss Dechamps up in Ocean View this morning."

I was relieved I didn't have to go see Ms. McDare; I preferred not to spend too much time over the Ocean View community if I could help it. All the fancy mansions and overt wealth put me on edge.

"Okay, just don't antagonize her," I said. "You know what she's like. Also, perhaps you and Nathaniel should go into town and speak with the other businesses there to see if we can borrow some kitchen time from someone."

Nathaniel nodded and placed a hand on Joy's shoulder. "That sounds like a sensible plan to me. It would do us good to get some air and stretch our legs. There's nothing else we can do around here, and besides, I need to get some supplies to fix that leaking roof in Hope's room."

"Right," I said, standing up. "We have our jobs to do today, so let's get on. The Angelos don't give up when we face a challenge!"

Charity yawned and pawed the brown bag of breakfast goods and then placed her furry chin on her paws. "I see someone wants to hang around the house today." I scratched her behind her ears and got a little *mrow* in return.

There was something else there, though, a vision. My link with Charity flared for a brief moment, and I saw the kitchen through the parlor door from Charity's point of view and knew that she wanted to stay behind to spy on Laney and the scene.

"Okay, girl, you can relax today. Noah and I will go out instead, won't we, boy?"

Noah stood up and wagged his tail.

"Before we go out," Nathaniel said. "I'll take Hope some of this breakfast. She was in a funny mood this morning. Even more snappy than usual."

I checked the date on my iPhone. "It's expected," I said. "We're only a week away from the anniversary."

"Oh," Nathaniel said. "I didn't realize."

The anniversary in question was of the day Hope lost her husband in the Vietnam War.

Rueben was a lieutenant in the US army and had gone back out for a second tour. He never came back. Ever since then, Hope had remained up in the tower, in the suite previously known as the Lover's Loft, and mourned her soul mate.

She rarely came out, preferring to stay in that cold, dark room, looking out to the ocean over the cliffside.

We usually took extra-special care of her during this time. But what with Greg's murder and the issue with the banquet, the timing couldn't be worse. Still, the Angelos pulled together as a family and we would get through this, I hoped.

"I'll go up and see her later when I'm back from Ocean View," I said.

"Thank you, Grace," Joy said, standing up and hugging me. "Don't forget the doggy bakes for Dechamps. Laney kindly brought them out of the kitchen last night. They're over there in the tin."

Joy pointed to the purple tin on the sideboard.

"Right then, I best get going before the tide comes in. I don't want to have to walk the long way around."

"I'll get some lunch in for when you're back," Joy said.

"I won't be here, I'm afraid. I have a meeting with Zach at noon and will grab something then."

Joy raised an eyebrow. She had often suggested I move on and find someone else.

It had been fifteen years since I lost my Samson.

The truth was that I still loved him and often felt his presence around me, but I had lost that awful pain that accompanied me for so long after, and Samson always said to me that I should find someone if anything happened to him.

We shared that sentiment, actually. With us both working for the police, we had agreed that if anything ever happened to either of us, the other one shouldn't ever be lonely. But with Noah and Charity with me, the bakery, and my sisters, I rarely had any time to be alone.

Though, I had to admit, I had on occasion missed the closer connection one had with a partner. Zach, however, was far too young. I had trained him since he was twenty-one, and besides, I didn't think he felt about me in that way.

"And no," I said to Joy, "it's nothing like that. It's purely professional."

With that, I grabbed the tin of doggy bakes, my ornately carved hiking stick, and my beloved aviator sunglasses, and left the house with Noah dutifully by my side.

We headed out of the house and walked along the winding path that started at the edge of our front garden and wound around and down the side of the cliff toward the Cove.

Noah, as ever, ran ahead of me, eager to get to the beach. The ocean was out, the tide receding, leaving the sand glossy and shimmering in the morning sunlight. When the tide was in, the water was a clear blue, hence the name Hemlock Cove. It really was a beautiful place, and at this time, in late fall, it was quiet and empty of tourists.

Noah and I had the beach to ourselves as we headed north toward the posh Ocean View gated community. As we walked on, approaching the steps that led up to the entrance, we came to a familiar place: Lovers' Rocks. A collection of huge boulders that created a kind of mini Neolithic maze one could walk through.

Noah had already rushed inside between the rocks, his paws leaving prints in the sand.

As I approached, however, my body stiffened.

My connection to him sharpened and it was if I had raised hackles on my back.

I focused my mind and entered his vision. My heart began to race, and from the corner of his view, I saw something move: a shadow, as though it were purposely hiding from us.

Noah growled and padded closer to the tall boulder the shadow had moved behind. I tried to call him back, but it was too late.

A dark figure stepped out from behind the rocks.

Chapter Four

"Abe? Abe King? Is that you skulking about there?" I said as I stepped into the shadows of the rocks.

"Yeah," he said, with a deep gruff voice that belied his youthful twenty-four years.

Noah ran up to him and jumped up on his hind legs, licking Abe's big, round face.

"Easy, boy," Abe said, making a fuss of the dog. Noah had always got on well with Abe.

"What are you doing out here on your own in that state?" I asked. I removed my aviators and gestured with them to his ripped shirt and pants.

Noah then got down and sat by my side, his tongue lolling out and tail wagging.

"Um, it's… a…"

"Is that lipstick on your neck?"

Although I asked, I knew it for certain. Abe's once-white shirt was open around the collar, showing his muscular neck upon which was a smearing of scarlet red lipstick. Given his torn clothes and his shoulder-length brown hair all fussed up, I didn't need to be a trained detective to guess what he had been up to.

"Let me guess," I said before Abe could speak. "You and Francesca Finch?" She was well known in the Cove for her bright red lips regardless of the occasion.

Although Abe towered over me, standing at least six

foot four and about that across his shoulders, his cheeks reddened with embarrassment.

He simply nodded and tried to hide the smile on his face.

The wind blew through the rocks and I smelled the unmistakable scent of the local Hemlock Cover Distillery's single malt scotch wafting from Abe.

"You two have a good night, did you?" I asked, and then before he could answer, added, "And was that before or after the fight in the Lucky Clover?"

"You know 'bout that, eh?"

"Only what Logan told me. What happened there?"

He shrugged those big shoulders of his. "Jus' one of those things, Grace. The old man's been having a few problems with Suzanne Manning."

"What kind of problems? Must be serious for you lot to be feuding in Greg Pelt's bar." I didn't mention that he had turned up in my bread oven.

"Just some deals, you know what them two are like; they'll fight over the color of the sky if one swore it was blue. They got arguing about her trying to muscle in on my family's logging contracts; then Matt got involved and started throwing fists…"

"So you and your brother stepped in to finish it off?" I prompted.

"Nah," he said, "Greg broke things up and threw us out before it got to that."

Although I don't have the ability to use witchcraft to tell if someone is speaking the truth, I can get a sense of someone's sincerity via Noah. He was watching Abe closely and I got no sense from him that he was concerned.

I leaned on my walking stick and stared up into Abe's eyes as I asked, "What did you do after that?"

"What do you mean?"

"After the fight, where did you go? Did you carry it on?"

"Nah, we all went our separate ways."

"But I'm asking you specifically, Abe. What did you do afterward?"

Abe ran a large paw of a hand through his thick hair, and he scrunched his eyes as the sun broke through a cloud and a beam struck his face through the rocks. He winced with pain, no doubt brought on by the scotch. "I stumbled over to Fran's place and fell asleep in her barn. I daren't go home drunk again; Mum would be furious with me."

"And you just slept there in the barn all night?"

"Well, no, Fran heard me snoring and took me up to her room… but hey, what's this got to do with you?" he said, finally realizing I was questioning him a little too much for casual conversation. Abe wasn't the sharpest needle in the sewing kit.

I decided to try him out. "Greg Pelt's dead. Someone killed him last night after he locked up the bar."

His jaw dropped open and he leaned over, placing his big paws on his thighs. "He's what? Dead? What the… you kidding me?"

"No, his body was found in my bread oven this morning. Given the timing, it seems that he was killed not long after closing up for the night." I continued to stare at him while also noting Noah's reactions. Nothing out of the ordinary came to me.

Abe's shock seemed genuine when he blurted out, "That poor sonofa… Sorry, that's awful news. I know we weren't best buddies, but… Wait, you think it was me?"

He stood up straight then and glared down at me.

I'd seen enough types like him not to be intimidated,

so I stared right back at him. “Well, was it you? Did you kill Greg Pelt for throwing you out of the bar? It's clear you were quite drunk.”

“No!” Abe shouted. “It wasn't me, Grace. How dare you? You've known me since I was a kid. How could you even think I was capable of that? Besides, like I said, I was with Francesca all night.”

“The police are going to want to check that, Abe. But for what it's worth, I do believe you.”

He shuffled past me, his face red but not with embarrassment this time. “I better go warn the rest of the family. It's clear you lot are going to point the finger at us.”

With that he stormed off across the beach in the long, loping gait of his.

I looked down at Noah, who raised an eyebrow at me and twitched an ear. “I think we've upset him. Okay, fine,

I've upset him, but I had to ask. Besides, this will be useful to Zach. Come on, old friend; let's get to moving. We've a rich lady and her Chihuahua to make happy with some fresh doggy bakes."

Woof!

*

We arrived at the driveway of Michelle Dechamps just as she was getting the post from her postbox. Despite the early hour, she was already wearing a designer white dress and her rich red hair nicely styled. Her makeup was flawless with pale skin tones and thick lashes.

"Morning, Michelle, I've got Fifi's bakes with me." I held up the tin to prove it.

Noah's eyes followed; no doubt he was hoping I'd drop the tin.

“Ah, Grace, you've come at the right time. It's almost Fifi's breakfast. Won't you come in for a coffee?”

Although it was phrased as a question, it was more of an order. Michelle spun on her heels and slinked her way around the brand-new Porsche in her drive before disappearing inside her huge white-fronted mansion.

Every house on the development looked the same: huge and opulent. The only thing that was different from place to place was the car brand. All top of the range, though: Ferrari, Jaguar, Mercedes, Lexus, and even a Rolls Royce.

Given my hiking boots, jeans, and old overcoat, I felt distinctly out of place.

Still, one did not say no to free coffee, especially from someone in Ocean View. At least you knew it would be the good stuff.

Once inside, Michelle gestured to a dining table. We

both sat down and she handed me the cup of coffee. It smelled divine. Noah slumped by my feet with a huff, feeling left out. I had already given Michelle the tin of doggy bakes, and she had dispensed a small handful to Fifi, who chowed down with tiny bites and a wagging eagerness.

"So," Michelle said to me, looking over her mug of coffee, "what's new in the world of the Angelos? Business going well?"

I could tell from the sparkle in her glacier-blue eyes that she already knew.

"It's been difficult," I said.

"The Greg situation?"

"Um, the dead Greg situation, yes. I assume you've heard about it already?"

She nodded and sipped her coffee. I did the same and looked away, suddenly feeling like she had only given me the coffee to get the gossip. She had already paid for the doggy bakes, so it wasn't like she owed me in that sense.

"I heard from Chris," she said. "You know, that stylist from Deb's? She's Laney's cousin."

"News certainly travels fast in this town," I said.

"Yeah, well, given that he was a total shit, it's not surprising."

Her reaction surprised me for a moment. In the three or so years I had known Michelle, I had never heard her swear before or show that kind of animosity toward anyone. Sure, she could be a bit cold in her ways, but never that passionate.

"What do you mean?" I asked. "Greg was okay."

"That bast… I mean, that man cheated on me!"

Well, that was a surprise indeed. I hadn't known she was seeing him. Michelle seemed like the eternal single lady to me: too busy with her business and investment career to need or want a relationship. "I didn't realize you two were together," I said before finishing my cup of coffee.

"It wasn't a long-term thing."

She looked hurt at this and stared down into her cup for a moment.

"I'm sorry," I said, "I don't mean to pry, but you can talk to me, if you want."

She took a handkerchief from her pocket and dabbed her eyes. I couldn't tell if she was crying or just acting. She sniffled then said, "We dated for a few months in secret until recently. I was finally beginning to have stronger feelings toward him when I found him sweating over one of his cheap barmaids."

"Sweating over?" I prompted. "As in—"

"Screwing her," Michelle snapped. "Right there in the office of his bar. The filthy cheat didn't even seem bothered that I had caught him at it."

"Did you know who the girl was?" I asked.

"That little tart, Casey Foster!"

"I'm so sorry," I said. "What happened after that?"

She looked at me as if I had slapped her. "I dumped him right there and then, of course. What else would you expect me to do? I do not suffer cheats!"

"So… you were angry with him?" I asked, easing my way toward the main question, but Michelle was already one step ahead of me.

"Of course I was, but no, I didn't kill him, although I can't say I was entirely upset about the news, but still, I wouldn't wish that on him. I would have settled for a maimed limb or something, but not murder. And before you ask me, I was nowhere near the bar or your bakery last night."

"I wasn't going to," I said. "I'm sorry to have upset you.

I didn't mean to pry."

She placed her mug on the table and reached out to cup my hands in hers. "It's fine, Grace. I'm just being all… highly strung. It's all come as a bit of a shock. Even poor Fifi has taken the news hard. Look at her, she's shaking!"

Noah looked at the smaller dog and made a huffing noise.

There was nothing wrong with Fifi. The reason why she was shaking was because she barely had any fur and the kitchen floor was made from stone tiles—not exactly the warmest of decor for such a little dog.

"So if you don't mind me asking," I continued, "where were you last night?"

"David Kings' garage. Getting some work done on a new project. A classic car I picked up from an artist in the Hamptons."

"That's an odd place to be late at night."

"It's true, it was odd. David called me just after midnight to ask me to go and see him. You see, he loves Mustangs and was working on the car late when he discovered a small problem and, before he did any more work, wanted me to okay it. I was awake, and well, truth be told, I was feeling lonely, so I decided to go out and see what the issue was. At the very least, it'd get me out of the house for a few hours."

I noted this in my mind and remembered then I was due to meet Zach at noon. I checked my watch and saw that I'd be at least an hour late if I didn't hurry up. It was much later than I expected and nearly noon. I was only supposed to drop the doggy bakes off and head straight over to the Bean and Broomstick.

"I'm sorry to cut the conversation short," I said, "but I must dash, I have a prior engagement." I reached for my phone in my coat pocket to call Zach, but I had left it back at the house. "And, sorry to be a pain, but would you mind if I borrowed your phone? I've left mine at home."

Michelle smiled kindly and pointed to a wall-mounted phone behind me. "Please, help yourself. I've got some important business to attend to myself. Are you okay letting yourself out? I'll be working in the front office."

"I'll be fine, thank you."

Michelle picked up Fifi and headed deeper into the mansion. I stood up and took the phone off the hook and placed it to my ear. A series of beeps indicated she had a voice message. I know I shouldn't have done it, but my old detective skills kicked in and acted out of instinct.

I listened to the previously listened-to messages, and she was right about David King. He had phoned Michelle around midnight last night to talk about some bodywork on her Mustang. Given that David King's garage was on the other side of town, Michelle wouldn't have been in the area at the right time.

I was glad, though; Michelle might be a little hard-nosed, but she was a good woman, and I did consider her a friend of sorts.

Putting that behind me, I dialed Zach's number. He answered on the second ring.

"Zach, it's me, Grace, I'm calling from Michelle Dechamps' house. Listen, I'm going to be a bit late for our meeting, I've lost track of time this morning."

"Oh, that's not like you," he said, "but it's okay. I'll enjoy the extra time and the extra cake."

"Good for you, you need fattening up."

"I'm fine as I am… athletic."

We both laughed. Zach was the least athletic man either of us knew.

"Listen," I said, "I've got some interesting information

for you, about Greg."

"That makes the two of us. I heard back from the ME of her initial findings. I think you're going to be interested in what she's discovered."

"I'll be there as soon as I can!"

Chapter Five

By the time I arrived in town I was already three-quarters of an hour late. I had rushed over, even though Zach had said not to worry about it; I hated being late. I turned into Main Street, the long road that cut through the town and featured the famous shopping boulevard.

We had everything there from candle shops, herb and spice importers to some of the best couture fashion boutiques outside of New York, although those were always too rich for me. Still, I got a buzz from looking at the dresses through the windows.

The fall colors gave the place a lovely atmosphere. Brown and yellow leaves lined the old cobblestones that were glossy with damp air. A chill breeze whistled through iron railings and around my neck, sneaking its way through any gaps in my scarf.

Noah curled around my leg, sheltering himself from the cold.

Despite the colder weather, Main Street was busier than I had seen it for some time, and the sidewalks were crammed with shoppers, many of whom I recognized. The odd thing was that they wouldn't acknowledge my greeting.

"Margery Thistle!" I called out as one of our neighbors bustled past without responding to me. Clearly the news about Greg Pelt had got out.

The small, hunched woman stumbled slightly and turned halfway round before shaking her head and scuttling off, mumbling something about my family and finding trouble.

It wasn't fair. This time, trouble had found us.

We hadn't asked to have a dead body turn up in our bread oven.

Noah made a low *harrumph* sound, showing his displeasure. I would have done the same if it were not for a tap on my shoulder, making me nearly jump out of my skin.

Spinning around, I saw Zach's tall frame peering over me, a tired expression on his face.

"You didn't sleep too well this morning, I take it?" I said, because stating the obvious seemed like the only polite response. The alternative would be to tell him what I thought of his creeping up on me, and seeing as the townsfolk didn't seem that enamored with me this morning, that would have had only aided their opinion.

Besides, a classy lady like myself does not swear in public. I save that for when I'm watching *Castle* or *The Mentalist* on TV and the detectives missed the freaking obvious clue. I know, I shouldn't get so caught up in these things, but old habits die hard.

"No sleep at all," Zach said finally. "I don't know if you heard, but there was an incident at your bakery last night."

"Touché," I said. "Well, let's get a gallon of espresso into your bloodstream."

After making a fuss of Noah, Zach nodded and led me across the street toward the Bean and Broomstick. The exterior was modeled in an old New England style, including a porch, on which were a number of old-fashioned broomsticks leaning against the facade.

The signage was hand painted and was starting to crack and flake away, which actually helped give it that authentic look. It really stood out too, because either side were glass-fronted boutiques—one a men's tailor's and the other a posh shoe shop featuring boots to die for in the window that I had lusted after for years.

As we were approaching fall, they seemed ideal. I looked down at my clunky hiking boots and felt a bit crappy about myself.

Zach must have seen my expression, as he nudged me in the side gently with his elbow.

"Hey," he said, "you'll get drool on the window. Besides, you look fine as you are." He accentuated the word 'fine'.

As I always did when he paid me a compliment, I brushed it off with comedy, this time by taking off my aviator shades and staring off into the middle distance as if I were some model out on a shoot. "You do talk a lot of sense occasionally, dear Zachary," I said.

"Only my mum calls me that," he said, ruining the moment.

Sure, I'm a few years older than him, but one doesn't appreciate being reminded that his mother wasn't much older.

"Coffee's on you," I said, pushing him through the door of the café. "And I'll have cake for the trouble."

Once inside, my mood instantly improved.

The decor was all dark wood and rustic chic. We took our usual spot in a booth at the rear of the dining area. A long bar stretched all the way across the rear of the café, behind which were a number of ancient-looking coffee machines all gleaming in their copper and chrome glory.

As we weren't long after Halloween, the place still had some of its decorations up: cobwebs in the corner, silhouettes on the wall of a pointy-hatted witch riding the stereotypical broomstick, and carved pumpkins in many of the nooks and crannies of the place.

The place was half full, many of who were tourists staying a few days longer after their Halloween trip. It was always easy to tell the outsiders from the locals—the tourists always had cameras with them, snapping every little detail that we locals probably took for granted and didn't notice anymore.

Noah showed no real interest. I thought he must have been tired after his walk on the beach and our rush over to town. He climbed up beside me on the leather seat and curled into a ball.

Usually pets weren't allowed in here, but since I had come here almost every other day for a decade, they had long gotten used to me being accompanied by Noah or Charity.

As long as they didn't cause a problem and as long as no one complained, they were allowed to stay.

"I thought you said you would be late," Zach said.

"I am," I replied, checking my watch. I held my wrist up to his face. "See, nearly 1 p.m."

Zach showed me his watch and it showed noon.

A young male server with black hair halfway down his face approached us and smiled. "Good to see you again, Ms. Angelo," he said, shyly moving his hair away from his eyes. "Detective Jackson, can I take your order?"

"Afternoon, Liam," I said. "Before we do, can you confirm the time for me?"

He checked the chunky leather-strapped watch around his wrist and said, "A couple of minutes to midday."

"Darn it," I said. "My watch has been slow all this time. I only had the battery replaced a few days ago from the miserable old watchmaker up the street. Cost almost as much as the watch and it clearly doesn't work properly!"

Zach just smiled and shook his head. "All that rushing around for nothing… still, at least it gives us time to go over a few things."

Feeling like an idiot, I ordered the coffees and a slice of spiced pumpkin cake with cream cheese frosting.

Sugar therapy would soon have me feeling better about making a fool of myself.

Liam took the order and a few minutes later brought the items to our table. When he left, Zach took a long gulp of his coffee and relaxed back into his seat. He then reached into his coat's inner pocket and brought out a piece of folded paper.

"What's that?" I said, cocking an eyebrow.

"The medical examiner's initial findings." He passed the sheet to me but continued, saying, "She has put the time of death at around 1:30 a.m. due to the nature of the clotting. Also, there's this."

He reached into his pocket again and passed me a printed photograph showing a grainy black-and-white scene. I could make out Greg walking down a narrow alley, his features lit by a lamp.

"Where was this taken from?"

"St. Anne's Avenue. You know, the alley that runs alongside the canal through the warehouse district."

"That's between the Lucky Clover and the Guesthouse," I said.

"Yup, and according to that timestamp, he was just ten minutes away from your place. I made that walk this morning and the times stack up. He would have been killed within a few minutes of arriving at your bakery."

I dug into my spiced pumpkin cake and thought about it. "I don't understand why he ended up in the oven," I said. "Sure, he could have passed by the back of the

Guesthouse if he were on his way home, but he would have had to get in first."

"True, and Laney confirmed there was no sign of forced entry."

"So what does that mean?" I asked. I had an idea, but I couldn't get out of the habit of schooling Zach, even though I had been out of the force for years and he had grown into a highly capable detective of his own standing.

"It means," he said, "that either someone left the back door unlocked, or someone had a key."

"Well, if they had a key, then this all seems premeditated. Given what we know about the fight and the pool of suspects so far, it doesn't sound planned at all."

Zach nodded then eyed my cake. I still had half the slice left.

I sighed and pushed the plate over. "Here, you have the rest," I said. "You look like a starving urchin in Victorian London."

"Thank you ever so kindly, ma'am!" he said in a terrible cockney accent and then took a big bite out of the cake.

"No one has a key," I said. "It was opportunistic. Someone clearly followed him home, as this photo shows. There must have been a struggle, and the killer, seeing an opportunity of an open door or something, panicked and dumped the body. It doesn't make sense to plan to put it into a bread oven—that's the behavior of someone who wasn't thinking straight, which in turn leads to the rationale of this being an opportunistic killing."

Crumbs fell down Zach's chin, covering his trench coat lapels.

I reached over and brushed them off. “Mucky boy,” I said, giving him a wink.

“I'd agree,” Zach said, “that this was an 'in the moment' incident, which brings us back to the Mannings and the Kings.”

Leaning back and clicking my fingers, I said, “Of course, my news, I totally forgot! On my walk up to Michelle Dechamps's place this morning, I stumbled across Abe King. He looked worse than you did.”

“In what way?”

I explained the whole conversation and how Abe had slept over at Francesca's place.

“That should be our first port of call, then,” he said. “What about Dechamps? You said you had news about her on the call earlier.”

Between sips of coffee, I filled Zach in on the entire situation about David King's voicemail message and the whole car situation.

Zach laughed and shook his head. "It's been one morning and you've already questioned two suspects. You don't hang around, do you?"

Shrugging my shoulders and smiling, I said, "Early bird gets the worm, Zach."

After another round of coffees and a bowl of water for Noah, we reached the end of our meeting. Zach stretched his arms and yawned then said, "We ought to divide the workload when it comes to questioning those involved with the fight last night. Who do you want, the Kings or the Mannings?"

"Who don't you want to deal with?" I asked.

"Well, Callum King has always been a royal pain in my butt..."

"He might look scary, but he's a pussycat, really."

"Sly and vicious?" Zach said.

"Your opinion of cats is disturbing," I said. "But it's fine, I'll go see Callum later today. He and his crew are working up at Thornwood Manor this week, clearing those downed trees from last week's storm. It's only a short walk from here, and on the way to Francesca's farm, I'll check on Abe's alibi."

"Fine with me," Zach said. "That leaves me with Matt and Suzanne Manning. Call me the minute you find anything else out. In the meantime, I'll have Laney continue her investigations at your bakery to see if she can figure out how they got into your kitchen."

We said our goodbyes and we both set off in different directions. I had a feeling today was going to be an interesting one, but I didn't quite realize just how interesting.

Chapter Six

Before I set off to Thornwood Manor, I decided to take a stroll down Main Street to allow my cake to digest properly. It wasn't good to go hiking over difficult terrain on a full stomach.

We passed some of the boutiques until we reached my favorite place in the whole of Hemlock Cove: Donatelli's Books, one of the oldest bookstores in all of America.

The owner, Dario, was a gorgeous man and the latest

in a long line of Donatellis to run the store, having taken it over from his father a few years ago after the old man finally died on his 100th birthday with a smile on his face.

The bookstore had a traditional display that looked like something out of a Dickens novel. The square paneled windows were sprayed with fake snow to add to the old-time feel.

The door chime rang out a merry tune as I stepped inside, Noah close by me.

My face prickled for a moment, the warmth of the store beating back the frosty air.

No one else was in the store apart from Dario, who was sitting in a comfy-looking armchair by a wood-burning stove.

He had a book open on his lap and looked intently interested in its contents.

Dario was just a few years older than me but had kept

himself in good health and had the physique of someone much younger. He still played squash to a high level.

Today, he was wearing a typical Italian suit: sharp and well-fitting.

His hair was black and swept back from his forehead, revealing a friendly face behind a pair of black plastic glasses, which he had worn for decades before they became popular and cool.

Seeing that I had entered the store, he shut the book and stood up, bowing at the waist.

“Good afternoon, ma'am,” he said in a deep baritone voice. “And how may I be of service to you on this cold December day?”

“Well, I was just going to browse, but seeing as you've been kind enough to ask, I wonder if you have the book I ordered last week?”

He smiled and his beautiful brown eyes sparkled in the

firelight. I blushed and looked away, realizing I was probably staring. But how could I help it? He was just so fine standing there, surrounded by wooden shelves crammed with books of all kinds.

Some soft blues music was playing in the background, and the place smelled of leather, age, and whiskey. Essentially perfect. I could live here, seriously. Noah had drifted off to a corner of the store where another dog was curled up in a soft doggy bed.

A white Staffordshire terrier saw Noah and wagged her little stubby tail. The two of them sniffed each other and lay down together and shared a bone.

Totally adorable.

"Jessie never seems happier than when Noah's here," Dario said. "Perhaps we should arrange a doggy date some time, take them for a walk together?"

My heart actually fluttered a little and I must have

blushed even more than usual. But I simply nodded and said calmly, "I would like that very much. I'll give you a call as soon as I'm free. Currently I'm a little busy with..." I trailed off, realizing I probably shouldn't say anything about the case yet.

"I understand," Dario said as he stepped away from the fire and headed up a couple of steps and reached behind a counter to retrieve a book wrapped in brown paper. "I heard about Mr. Pelt. That must have been quite the shock for you."

"It wasn't the best thing to wake up to," I said, joining him at the sales counter. "Detective Jackson has hired me as a consultant, so I'm going to be busy for a while, but once that's done, I would be delighted to go on a doggy date with you."

"Splendid," he said, smiling wide.

He really was quite the handsome man. "Is this the

book?" I asked, stupidly pointing at the package in his hands that clearly looked like a book.

"Yes," he said, handing it over to me. "It came in this morning, actually. You must have had one of your feelings."

"Um…" I said, feeling awkward.

It always felt that way when someone brought something up that spoke of my witchy background and abilities. I tried not to confirm the rumors, but I guess they had been associated with me for so long, they just became who I was in the eyes of the Hemlock Cove citizens.

"I'm sorry," he said, picking up on my discomfort.

He touched my wrist with his free hand. Warmth seeped into me, traveling up my arm and all around my body until I no longer felt awkward.

An inner calm spread throughout me as though I had

just been hugged by the best cup of coffee in the world.

"How did you...?" I started, but the look in my eyes told me more than words could ever explain. He simply smiled and let go, handing me the book. In that moment, I knew there was more to my old friend Dario than I had previously known—that he was like me.

"Please, consider the book a gift," he said. "You'd do me a great honor."

As I was wrapped in that gooey blanket of calm, I didn't object. "Thank you, Dario, I really appreciate it. I shall snuggle up with it tonight. I've been waiting a long time to read this, Hercule Poirot's last case."

"I'm sure you won't be disappointed," he said, and I wasn't exactly sure what he was referring to, but it sounded good to me regardless.

"It's a bit sad, though, coming to the end after all these years following his cases."

"Indeed, but we're never too old to start something new."

The calm was giving way to other feelings, so I decided to take that as my cue to leave and head up to Thornwood Manor.

I said my goodbyes and left a doggy treat for Jessie. Noah and I spent the next thirty minutes hiking through woodland trails and up hills until we eventually arrived at the manor house.

Much like the architecture in Main Street, the house was very old and in traditional New England style. It was surrounded by ten acres of ancient woodland, hence the name of Thornwood, which also happened to be the name of the family who owned the place.

They'd been here for almost as long as my family, settling in Hemlock Cove less than a decade after my family had helped found it officially.

Despite the chilly weather, I was warm after the exercise of the hike and was a little sweaty by the time I reached the end of the gravel drive and knocked on the great white door with its iron knocker.

I knew Callum King was here, as I heard him yelling at his staff in the distance. I also saw his work truck in the parking area behind the house as Noah and I approached.

The door opened and a young teenage girl appeared in the space.

"Yeah?" she said, chewing gum and slouching there, her hands in her jeans pockets.

"I'm here to see Callum. I understand he's working in the woods today. May I speak with him?"

"Yeah," she said, unmoving, still chewing.

"Yeah to what? That he's here or I can speak to him?"

She shrugged. "Whichever you want. You wanna come

in so's I can fetch him?"

Not waiting, she turned her back and disappeared into the far reaches of the house.

Before I could step inside, the girl's mother appeared and smiled when she saw me. She was dressed in a lovely floral dress of white and scarlet, which complemented her shoulder-length red hair. "Grace," she said, beaming wider. "So nice to see you again, won't you come in?"

She kissed me on the cheek and stepped back to allow me in.

"It's good to see you too, Stephanie," I said. We knew each other reasonably well, often bumping into each other at various town gatherings, fairs, and charity events. "Is Noah okay in here?" I asked, remembering she was particular about her home.

"Of course. How could I resist that little face?"

She bent down and rubbed behind his ears, making

baby talk. I could tell Noah was not impressed—he sent me a vision of his annoyance.

"What do I owe this pleasure?" Stephanie Thornwood said.

"I'm afraid it's not a social call," I said. "I've come to speak with Callum."

She stood up straight and motioned for me to follow her. She led me through the house and out into the rear conservatory. Callum was there, sitting at a table, enjoying a mug of tea. His sons were outside, tending to the logging machinery.

"You have a guest," Stephanie said to Callum with an air of curiosity.

Callum looked up, smiled, and then became still. Eventually, he put the mug of tea down slowly and asked Stephanie for privacy, which she duly obliged.

"I guessed I'd be talking to you… or Zach," Callum

said, gesturing to the empty wicker chair at the small round table. His face resembled an old tree with its deep crags and tanned color.

Some of the kids around town called him 'Old Tree Man' and not just because he ran a family logging business.

Even his shaggy, thinning, brown hair resembled a mess of twigs and branches. He smelled of sawdust and was mostly covered in it, the pale yellow fluff stuck on his thick sweater.

"You've not gone to see anyone at the station," I said, sitting down, "so I'm presuming you know what this is about and that you're going to say you know nothing about it?" I didn't say this with any malice. Callum was the kind of guy who preferred people to get straight to the point, which I appreciated, as it saved a lot of time.

Noah padded around the conservatory, sniffing as he

went, as though he were on his own private case.

Callum eyed him suspiciously before turning his attention back to me.

"You know I've got contacts in town," Callum said, his voice croaky and shaky, the vocal quality of a man who had been shouting and hollering out in all weather for most of his sixty-plus years. "I heard about Greg as soon as I woke this morning. It's a damned shame."

"He threatened your family and the Mannings with a shotgun last night, didn't he? To break up a brawl."

"So? You think I'd kill a man for that? You know how many people have pointed a gun at me over the years? If I killed every man who did that, I'd be a notorious serial killer. It's just how Greg was. Especially lately, always wound up, rising to every little thing."

"It's not just that, though," I said. "There was the thing with Joanne, your youngest daughter. She worked behind the bar with Greg for a while, didn't she, along with Casey Foster?" I had remembered what Michelle had said and couldn't help but use that to get Callum to open up, but I wasn't expecting quite his reaction.

Chapter Seven

Callum launched to his feet with surprising agility. He towered over me, his face red with rage. "What are you saying? Why bring Joanna into this? Just who the hell do you think you are, Grace?"

I put my hands in front of me to calm Callum down. "I'm not saying anything, I'm just asking questions. I know about Greg and Casey, did he also… you know, with Joanna? Is that the reason she no longer works there?"

Callum ran a trembling hand through his hair and spun away. Then back to me he said, "Pelt had it coming, you know that? Couldn't keep his damned hands to himself. But that's none of your business, Grace, and I don't appreciate you coming to my place of work hassling me and throwing around accusations."

He stepped forward, but then suddenly stopped as Noah appeared by my side and growled deep in his throat. He bared his teeth and, despite being the most lovable chocolate lab in the world, still managed to look intimidating enough to make Callum back away.

"I'm sorry, I'm sorry," he said. "Get that thing away from me."

I patted Noah on the side of his belly. "Good dog," I said. "Stay here."

Taking a deep breath to steady myself, I forced

calmness upon me and responded to Callum as best I could. "I get you're upset, but I've not accused anyone. I'm just asking questions to understand what has happened. I'm trying to help you, Callum. Right now, it doesn't look good, does it?"

"And what do you mean by that?"

"You and your sons, along with Suzanne and Matt Manning, were the last people to see Greg before he was killed. He threatened you with a gun. On top of that, he had an affair with your youngest daughter, who you're naturally protective of."

"You saying I killed that lowlife?"

I shrugged. "Did you?"

For a brief moment he tensed as though he struggled to remember if he had or not. Then, the confusion disappeared and he was his domineering self once more. "No, Grace, I did not kill Gregory Pelt, and neither did any of my family."

"So where were you after Greg threw you out of the bar?" I asked, deciding to keep pushing while he was still being cooperative.

He flared his nostrils and gritted his jaw before saying, "I was sleeping with my wife. All night. I went straight home. You can ask her yourself if you don't believe me. Now with that explained, I've got work to do, so we're done here, Grace, and don't think I'll forget about this anytime soon."

Callum stormed out of the conservatory to join his sons.

"Well, that was interesting," I said to Noah. "I guess we ought to go."

I briefly looked around for Stephanie Thornwood, but I couldn't find her and I didn't want to go snooping around the mansion, so Noah and I left through the front door and headed down the long gravel path toward the northwest edge of Hemlock Cove.

Francesca Finch's farm was only about a thirty-minute walk away, and although it was reaching late afternoon, it wasn't quite dark yet, so I decided it'd be worth stretching my legs one more time that day.

It would also give me time to process the whole situation with Callum.

The case looked pretty complicated at that point, with lots of people connected, but I had faith something would click and it would all make sense.

Before I reached Francesca's farm, however, I stopped off at a phone booth and called home to find out how Joy was getting on with finding new premises. She answered almost immediately.

"Angelo's Bake & Cake," she said, using her customer-facing voice, all upbeat and cheerful.

"Joy, it's me, Grace. How's things going? Any luck so far?"

Her voice changed instantly to one heavy with disappointment. "None yet," she said with a deep sigh. "I've called all the restaurants and bakeries in the Cove, and either they didn't want to have anything to do with us because of poor Greg, or they were too busy themselves. I really don't know what we're going to do."

"Could we perhaps use non-industrial ovens? If we got all the neighbors together, perhaps that could work?"

"I already spoke with the ones closest to us..."

It didn't take Poirot to figure out what the answer was.

This was one of the trickier aspects of being known 'witches' within the town. Although most people were friendly enough to us in the streets or at events, beneath it all there was a mistrust that we could never seem to dispel.

"There's one other option," Joy said.

I didn't like where this was leading, as I had a feeling she might go down this route. "What exactly do you have in mind?" I asked.

"I've been working on this concoction. It's a mix of herbs and plant extracts that I found in Mum's old journal."

"Joy…" I warned, "I thought we had already agreed never to go there?"

"But, Grace, this is a desperate time. We could lose our business."

I looked through the misted-up glass of the phone booth and saw Noah staring back. His ears had folded down and his furry eyebrows were furrowed.

I got the sense from him that, like me, he too disapproved.

After all, I did believe that even though he was a dog,

he had the essence of my father's soul within him, and he more than anyone knew the trouble that would come from resurrecting Mum's old spells and experiments.

"Grace?" Joy said. "Are you still there?"

"Yes, sis, I'm here, and I can't agree to this plan of yours. We can't use your gift to influence people. How would that go down with the Cove residents? They're suspicious of us already. That would only confirm things. Besides, remember what happened to the Guesthouse when Mum started using her abilities to increase the bookings and people's happiness of their stay?"

The line went silent and I pictured Joy looking around the place, seeing how it was almost falling apart and a pale shadow of its former glory.

The problem with using influencing spells was that it always came back with an equal reaction. Magic was much like science in that respect; you couldn't disrupt nature and expect there to be no consequences.

I heard Joy sigh with resignation. "Okay," she said eventually. "I know you're right, but I'm just so worried. This was our biggest contract, and if we lose it, we won't have any work until the New Year. We missed out on all the other winter business to be able to meet McDare's banquet requirements."

"I know, sis, but trust me, using your ability to fix it isn't the way. At least not like that. We need to be cleverer than that. Listen, I've got to talk with Francesca Finch, and then I'm done for the day. Why don't I order a takeout meal and we'll discuss this when I get back? We'll figure something out, I'm sure."

"As long as it's Chinese food," she said.

"Consider it done. I'll order yours and Nathaniel's favorite. We could all do with some cheering up. Okay, sis, I should go before it gets too late. I'll see you soon.

And don't worry. We're going to fix this."

"Thanks, Grace. And don't be out too late! There's a killer out there."

"I'll be safe, I promise. Bye!"

I put the phone back on its hook and removed my phone card. I felt a real chill in the air when I stepped out of the booth, and I didn't think it was just because of the cool December temperatures. It was also the realization that Joy was right—there *was* a murderer out here somewhere.

Gripping my walking cane tighter, ready to use it as a club if needed, I headed off to Francesca's with Noah close by my side. His ears were up and his body language alert.

We managed to get to Francesca's without being attacked, so I chalked that one up as a win.

Her farm was decorated as it always was during

winter: with fairy lights around the two tall oak trees that stood in front of the old house. The barn next to the house had a pair of sycamore trees with more lights, which obscured a pile of what looked like tractor parts and tools strewn about the place.

"Pretty, isn't it, Noah?" I said as we opened the gate and approached the front door.

The doorbell was surrounded with a small ivy garland, and a small glowing Santa sat to one side with a jolly face. I was still smiling when the door opened.

The light of the kitchen bathed Francesca. She was wearing a leather apron around her impossibly thin body. It struck me then what an odd couple she and Abe would make: he the giant and she the petite little thing.

"Grace Angelo?" Francesca said. "What can I do for you?"

Her shining brown hair was tied back in a ponytail,

and some flour dusted her nose and chin.

"I hope I'm not interrupting," I said. "You look pretty busy with baking."

She looked at her hands; I saw that they too were covered in flour. "Oh, it's fine, just making some mince pies and cinnamon rolls. Is there anything I can do for you?"

"I was hoping I could talk with you about last night. You see, I saw Abe this morning and he said that he—"

"Was with me last night? Yeah, that's right, and we're not ashamed to admit it."

This sudden defensiveness caught me off guard, but I gathered my train of thought and pressed on. "May I come in and ask you a few questions? It's about Greg Pelt. I'm here as a consultant to Detective Jackson."

She dropped her hands by her sides and her eyes widened ever so slightly.

I had learned that this wasn't an unusual response, a kind of calm surprise.

She stepped back and waved Noah and me into her home, leading us into the kitchen.

"Tea?" Francesca offered, pointing to a pot already on the rustic pine kitchen table.

The kitchen itself was one of those gorgeous old farm-style ones with a range oven, green tiled walls, and big chunky wooden worktops.

"Thanks," I said.

Francesca sat opposite me and poured two cups.

Noah was sat under the table by my feet. Something was bothering him, I could sense, but I wasn't quite sure. He wasn't quite ready to tell me, so I left him to do his thing.

"So," Francesca said, "what is it you want to know, and in what capacity?"

I appreciated her attitude and getting right down to it, so I decided to take the blunt approach too. "Did you know that last night, well, early this morning, Gregory Pelt was murdered and his body was found in one of my ovens?"

"Yes, I heard. Abe called me shortly after he had spoken with you."

My first thought was whether it was to get their story straight, but she continued on.

"I know you must think I'm giving him an alibi, but what he said was true. Abe was pretty drunk by the time he came here. I heard some noise in the barn, and when I went out, I found him there, passed out on a bale of hay."

"Is that normal?"

"For the general public? No. But Abe has crashed there a few times. He's harmless, so I often just let him sleep here if he's been on the ale. He doesn't cause any problems and often does a few jobs around the place for me."

"But last night was different. You didn't leave him out there, did you?"

Francesca blushed and looked down at her cup of tea. She nodded and mumbled, "No."

I could feel Noah shuffling around beneath the table, sniffing something that had got his attention. I couldn't really connect with him directly while also concentrating on questioning Francesca, so I let Noah be for a moment and carried on.

"What time was this?" I asked.

"It was about twelve thirty when he first arrived. I actually saw him coming up the path. I knew how cold it was out last night, so I went out and brought him inside. He was a little drunk, and I was afraid he would get pneumonia or something."

Thinking over the timeline, if it were true that he was here at midnight, he wouldn't have had time to get back to the alley where Greg was attacked and then stuffed the body in the oven.

"So what happened then? Did he stay all night?"

She looked down again, appearing demure, which contrasted with her earlier defensiveness.

"Yeah. He left here around 6:30 a.m. I made him eggs. Grace, listen, we don't want this becoming public knowledge. It's just a fling, nothing serious, you understand? Abe's a good guy, but neither of us wants a relationship. We just occasionally…"

"Hook up, I think the kids say these days?"

"Yes. That's the gist of it."

While she sipped the final contents of her tea, I moved my attention to Noah and realized what it was he was sniffing. I got the sense of it as though I were smelling it myself. It made me dizzy, and for a brief moment I had to lean against the table to keep my balance.

The smell was acidic, artificial, like something from an industrial process.

I couldn't quite pinpoint what it was, so I returned my attention back to Francesca. "Is there any way you can both corroborate you were here all night? I'd really rather be able to go back to Detective Jackson with something that can rule you both out of the investigation."

Francesca's cheeks reddened. "Well… there is, actually, but it's quite embarrassing."

"If it eliminates you both from the investigation, I'm sure it'll be worth it. Besides, I won't judge. You know me, Fran, I'm not like that."

"I know. Okay then."

Francesca reached into her jeans pocket and retrieved her cell phone. She flicked her fingers across the touchscreen a few times and handed it over to me.

The picture on display showed Francesca and Abe in a hug, smooching. Abe's arm was just in shot, showing that it was he holding up the phone to capture the 'selfie' shot.

At first I didn't understand how this would necessarily corroborate her story, but then I saw it: a clock in the background. It showed the time as a quarter to one in the morning, confirming Abe's whereabouts.

"Do you mind if I email this photo to my phone? I can give this to Detective Jackson to eliminate you both from the investigation. I'll tell him that it is sensitive."

"I guess that's okay. And if that's all?"

I wrapped up my investigation, thanked Francesca, and headed home in a taxi.

The day's events had taken its toll but at least I had a Chinese meal waiting for me. I would need it in order to piece together the case so far.

Chapter Eight

The Chinese meal had wiped us all out, and we sat around the parlor, nursing full bellies. Even Hope had allowed us to take some food up for her, although she had refused to join us.

Laney had left some time around 9:00 p.m., after getting a call from Zach to say that they'd got all they could from the crime scene. I thought this news might cheer Joy up, but although our kitchen was no longer a crime scene, the oven was still the site of poor Greg's corpse.

There was no amount of oven cleaner that could make that right.

"I can't use it," Joy said, leaning against Nathaniel on the chaise lounge. "It's just not right. What would the town say if it got out we were baking cakes and pies in a murder oven?"

"That our cakes are to die for?" I said.

Nathaniel winced at my bad joke. Joy just shook her head in disapproval. Even Noah looked at me as though I had just farted in church.

"I'm sorry," I said. "It's just been a long day. I wasn't thinking."

Feeling bad about making fun of a terrible situation, I excused myself from the room and went into the kitchen to boil a cup of herbal tea. Joy made this wonderful blend that helped you get to sleep. In some quantities it could be classified as a tranquilizer.

In fact, some of our ancestors who had pioneered the recipe had used it as such. They used to sell it in the marketplace as a 'bottled spell'. It was usually sold to lawmen looking for non-violent ways to arrest dangerous criminals, but eventually it was used by all kinds of people for all kinds of uses.

That was back in the day when our family was slightly less cautious about their witchcraft. These days, however, we were much more careful about what we used our powers for. Ultimately, it was that caution that helped us survive in Hemlock Cove for as long as we have.

My grandparents were the first to pitch the Angelos as friends to the town, offering their services as healers and scryers. My parents carried that tradition with the Guesthouse, but sadly, my mother, Charity, fell a little to the dark side, hence why the business of the Guesthouse failed and we changed to using the kitchen as a bakery.

Joy's herbal and spice knowledge was second to none and she used the skills to create delicious, and surprisingly healthy, vitamin-rich cakes. And of course, the herbal tea.

I had just finished brewing a pot when Noah started to bark.

"Someone's at the door," Nathaniel said from the parlor. "I'll get it."

"It's okay, I'll get it," I said. "I'm already up."

Nathaniel smiled and thanked me. I opened the door to find Zach standing there, looking all wiry and disheveled as ever.

He leaned in a little and sniffed a couple of times. "Mmm, smells like egg-fried rice and sweet and sour chicken. I hope there's some left. I'm starving!"

"Actually, there is," I said. "Want to come in?"

"Sure, thanks."

Zach came in, greeted the others, and petted Noah, who was like his best buddy whenever Zach came around. I made him take a seat and served up the leftovers we had kept. He tucked into them as though he hadn't eaten for a week.

"This is delicious," Zach said. "Where did you get it from, The Golden Dragon?"

"That's the one," Joy said. "Although, I added some of my own spices to give it a bit more seasoning and flavor."

"I hope I'm not going to sprout wings or something," Zach said and smiled mischievously.

"Just the tentacles… so, to what do we owe the pleasure of your visit?" I asked, eager to know what he had found out during the day.

Before Zach could start, Joy and Nathaniel said goodnight and went up to bed in order to give us some privacy. We weren't strictly supposed to share details of the case with anyone who wasn't approved by the DA's office.

When they had gone, I sat on the chaise opposite Zach and waited for him to start.

"I began my investigations with Suzanne Manning," he said. "It took half the day just to track her down. Eventually I found her at the harbor master's office, discussing their fishing license for the season."

"I can't believe that old jalopy of a boat is still seaworthy."

"Matt takes good care of it, apparently. Suzanne gave me an alibi. She told me she was at the Nightshade Diner shortly after she left the bar. Her daughter works there and corroborated it."

"Well, that's to be expected, isn't it? The Mannings all stick together. Her daughter would have given her an alibi whether she was there or not."

"Sure, but I have an officer talking with the manager of the bank opposite the diner. They have a security camera out front with an angle that would show us if Suzanne had, in fact, spent the evening there. I should get the results of that back some time tomorrow."

"So what did Suzanne say about the feud in the bar? Anything to make us think she might be involved with Greg's murder?"

Zach took the last bite of his meal and dabbed his chin with a napkin. "She didn't say a whole lot, really. It was the same old stuff, about how the Kings were using their influence to win contracts from the town planning department and keeping her family from expanding. You know how it is with those two."

And I did. The Mannings and Kings had been business rivals for decades, as they both vied for the positions as most influential family in the town, at least commercially. I liked to think that our history gave us Angelos some sway in things.

After I questioned Zach some more, and not coming up with anything else, I remembered my conversation with Francesca and showed him the photo that seemed to give her and Abe an alibi.

"Interesting," Zach said, looking at my phone. "I'll email this to my guys at the lab to look into. It seems legit, but you can never be sure. At the very least, it'll eliminate Fran and Abe from the investigation."

I told Zach about my interview with Callum, and he wasn't too surprised by the older man's reaction. Zach had had many similar experiences over the years.

Once we had both fully updated each other on our day's work, I asked, "So what now? This is your case, Zach, what do you want me to do next to help you out?"

I wasn't lacking direction; I knew where I wanted to go next, but I reminded myself that my capacity was that of a consultant and not the investigator of years past. It wasn't my responsibility to direct things.

“Well,” Zach said, passing my phone back to me, “I'm going to be in Salem most of the day tomorrow at the lab, going through the latest results, so if you're free, there are still some more suspects I'd like you to interview.”

“Sure, who have you got lined up for me?”

Checking his notebook, Zach said, “David King is next on my list if you're happy to handle him?”

“I can do that. I get on quite well with young David, and I wanted to talk with him anyway to check Michelle Dechamps's story about visiting his garage late at night to work on her car.”

“Sounds like a plan, then,” Zach said with a smile. He sat back and sighed as he sank into the chair. I could tell he was tired, as he looked even more drawn than usual.

I was about to ask him if he wanted me to get him some of Joy's rejuvenation tea when a crash from the kitchen startled the both of us.

Noah sprang up from his position by the side of Zach's chair and, tail wagging, dashed into the kitchen.

Charity, who I hadn't noticed before, darted out from beneath the coffee table and followed Noah. When I stood, the feeling of vertigo nearly unbalanced me.

A strong sense of concern from Charity hit me and I knew instantly what had happened in the kitchen. I headed through the parlor and into the kitchen. “Hope, is that you?” I asked, speaking into the darkness.

Before I got a response, I spun round to turn on the lights. Zach had joined me, and we both turned to see Hope standing in front of the oven, hunched over, her hand pressed against the brushed-steel surface.

She looked like a fragile bird with her thin arms and legs and her bright silver hair. Although she looked weak, I knew that she held strength unparalleled within her.

Ever since she lost her husband in the Vietnam War, she has remained heartbroken, living with the grief every single day.

And yet, despite that, she still managed to cut us down with her sharp wisdom and observations. When she spoke, we had no choice but to listen. Especially as those words were becoming ever more rare these days.

Only the people that came to her to have their hearts mended were treated to any kind of lengthy dialogue. Hope Angelo was known throughout Essex County for her ability to heal people's love wounds. In fact, she could seemingly heal everyone's apart from her own.

"Hope?" I said quietly, not wanting to startle her. It

was rare enough for her to leave her room and even rarer to see her in the kitchen like this, doing her… well, we called it 'channeling'.

Noah sat down and placed his chin on his outstretched paws.

Charity paced around Hope's legs and eventually settled beside her, her white tail flicking in the air.

Zach looked at me with a question written across his face.

I just shook my head and indicated with a finger over my lips for him to be quiet. It wasn't wise to break Hope out of her channeling. She had a short fuse at the best of times, but to pull her out suddenly would only lead to a furious reaction.

Growing up, I had been on the end of her sharp tongue more times than I could remember.

Hope did snark as well as anyone I had ever met, so

she had to be handled with care.

There was nothing for it but to wait.

Eventually, after what seemed like an hour, Hope pulled her hand away from the oven and turned slowly to face us.

She reached out a bony finger and pointed to me. Her eyes shone with an inner light that made Zach gasp. “You know who did this,” she said to me. “Look inside.”

“What do you mean, sis?” I asked.

“You have ears, girl. You heard me,” she snapped.

“Ms. Angelo,” Zach started, “do you have some information on what happened to Greg Pelt?”

Hope turned her attention to Zach, her face inscrutable. “He was killed and shoved into the oven, you silly man.”

Charity mewed a kind of admonishing tone. Hope bent down and scratched Charity behind the ears. “It had to be said," she said. "What a stupid question."

Picking Charity up and holding her close to her chest, Hope shuffled past us and headed upstairs. Zach just stared at the empty space she had just occupied. Then, turning to me, said, "What on earth was that all about? What did she mean that you know who did this?"

"Who knows? She's often obscure, but this is just bizarre."

But despite that, I felt like Hope had hit on something. I could sense something within my subconscious trying to come to the surface; some kind of connection that I was missing.

"Let me sleep on it," I said. "I'll call you tomorrow after I've spoken with David King."

"Okay," Zach said. "I best get home anyway. I need to be in Salem early. Take care, Grace."

"You too, Zach."

I walked him to the door and watched him drive up the road into the night.

When I came back in, I realized I hadn't given him one of Joy's herbal tea blends. I looked down at Noah, who had padded out of the kitchen to sit at the base of the chaise.

"Well, boy, I guess we better sleep on it, unless you have some answers? Did you have any clue what Hope meant?"

Noah's eyebrows just raised and lowered once, indicating to me that he, too, had no idea.

That night, my sleep came in fragments as I tried to figure out the meaning behind Hope's words. Nothing came to me, however, and I eventually fell into a deep sleep with a sense of dread pervading my dreams. I had a feeling that tomorrow would lead to a breakthrough one way or another.

Chapter Nine

The next morning, I woke early and joined the rest of the family in the kitchen.

As ever, my two shadows, Noah and Charity, were in lockstep with me. I always made sure that they were fed first; otherwise they would bug me until they were. Which was fair enough, I supposed, it wasn't as though they were just ordinary pets, after all.

Joy was still in her dressing gown, and Nathaniel

looked as if he hadn't slept for a decade, the bags under his eyes swollen and grey.

"Good morning, little sister," Joy said, peering through the rising steam from the kettle. The purple color of the steam told me that Joy had been brewing up some new concoction.

"Morning, you two," I said. "What's in the kettle? Smells a bit like… turmeric?"

"That's part of it," Nathaniel said, screwing up his face as though he had just taken a deep breath of a dirty diaper.

As I sat down on a stool at the breakfast bar, I had a bad feeling about all of this. Sure, the atmosphere was bound to be strained given the fact that only a day ago we had a body decomposing in our oven, but still, I could tell there was something else going on.

"You're not making a persuasion potion, are you, Joy?"

I asked, having remembered our phone conversation from the day before.

Joy stood up straight and thrust her chin out in defiance. "Of course not! What do you take me for, sis? I had agreed already that I wouldn't go down that route, hadn't I?"

"Yes, Joy, you did, but what on earth is it you're making?"

For a brief moment she didn't say anything, but given how tight her shoulders were and how her blue eyes sparkled, just as they always did when she was up to something out of the ordinary, it didn't take Columbo to figure out it wasn't any ordinary herbal remedy.

"Joy?" I prompted, using my stern face that had no effect whatsoever on my older sisters. I sometimes wondered if they had made some potion to combat its effects.

"If you must know, Mrs Nosey, it was a recipe pointed out to me. Hope had been digging through one of Mum's old books and—"

I stood up from my stool and placed my hands on my hips, trying to channel more of my disagreement through my failing 'stern face'. "Mum's books? Haven't we already talked about this? Don't you remember the last time Hope had you make something from those damned books? We conjured enough unruly spirits to chase off the last of the guests that stayed in this place."

Nathaniel ran a hand through his greying hair and sighed with a resignation that he was about to be caught up in one of the famous Angelo rows. They didn't happen very often, but when they did… well, things often went badly wrong.

"Now listen here, Grace," Joy said, pointing at me. "You may be the only one of us that has had a career in the police force, but that doesn't give you the right to control what goes on here. Mum's books have more in them than you give her credit for, isn't that right, Charity?"

The fluffy white cat that I was convinced held the spirit, or some aspect of it, of our mum jumped up onto the breakfast table, knocking her way through the bowls of cereal, and meowed loudly as though she were confirming what Joy was saying.

Noah woofed a couple of times as though he, too, were in agreement.

"I'm quite outnumbered on this one, aren't I?" I said. Charity walked under my chin, making sure to tickle me with her white tail.

"Fine," I said, crossing my arms over my chest. "I'll listen. Tell me, what is it that you're brewing, and what doom will it bring down upon us? It's not like we haven't had enough bad luck lately."

Joy shook her head, making her big white-blonde curls wobble. “Snark doesn't suit you, little sis. Leave that to Hope. She's had a lifetime to perfect it.”

“And doesn't give a damn,” I added.

“That may be so, but for some reason I'm yet to understand, she's decided to help us in our current predicament. This mix was an experimental one and never actually finished. But… I think I have figured it out.”

“Put me out of my suspense. What is this recipe supposed to achieve? And should I prepare myself for an infestation of ghouls?”

Nathaniel shuddered. “Don't. I remember the last one. It took me two weeks to clear up the mess.”

“No,” Joy said. “It's not a resurrection spell. It's a good fortune one, but one that can actually be targeted, which should take some of the risk out of the equation.”

My stomach tightened a little with anxiety. In my experience, trying to force good fortune or wealth often backfired, especially if used in a selfish manner. The universe was all about balance, and if one took too much, then there would be a debt to pay.

Joy must have seen my hesitation because she reached out and took my arm. "It's okay, trust me. I was up all night reading Mum's notes and seeing where she went wrong."

Charity gave a displeased *merp* at that.

"No offense," Joy said, tickling Charity behind the ears. "I just meant I've discovered a way of focusing it so it negates any potential downsides."

"Okay," I said, releasing a heavy breath, realizing it was too late for me to talk her out of it. "What's the aim of this spell?"

"Simple," Joy said. "It's a spell to bring good fortune to

our lives with regards to the oven. Having exhausted all other options to bake for the banquet elsewhere, there's only one option: we do it here."

"But we can't use the current oven, obviously," Nathaniel added.

"So," Joy continued, "the spell is to bring us a new solution. What that will be, I'm not yet sure, but according to Mum's notes, by using a mix of homegrown ingredients it's possible to address a particular problem. She says that problems have their own energy and can be directed."

"I really don't like the sound of this," I said.

Sure, she was right that problems, or any kind of negative effect, had its own energy, but by nature, that energy wasn't positive.

Generally, when we used a spell to banish bad feelings, thoughts, or in the case of the ghoul situation, entities, the negative energy was focused into a void, kind of like how heat was transferred into a heat sink.

To actually then direct that into the opposite, positive direction could lead to a doubling of the original issue.

"We could end up with more dead… things in our kitchen appliances," I said.

Joy smiled with a smugness that almost blinded me. "That's where my genius comes in!"

"Modest too," I said.

"Pfft, have faith, Grace. This cynicism doesn't suit you. I've been working on a new herb mix for the last few months, and it will suit this application perfectly. Trust me."

"So once this thing is all boiled up, what then?" I asked. Admittedly, curiosity had dampened my initial concerns. It wasn't often I saw Joy this animated, which meant, or at least I hoped it did, that she was genuinely onto something.

"I'll be mixing the solution with some items that Laney kindly gave me so I can focus the spell."

Oh no, this didn't sound good. "Items?" I said, not sure I wanted to know what she meant.

"Nothing that will compromise the case," Joy said. "So anyways, the spell components combined with the… items will hopefully help convert the negative energies of Greg's murder into a positive outcome, which should then give us the fortune to fix our problem with the banquet."

"That's a lot of shoulds and hopefulness," I said. I couldn't help but be skeptical. Sure, Joy had in the past earned a great deal of respect from other witches around the world with her research and sharing of information, but a lot of that was theoretical.

The problem with a good fortune spell mixed with an

energy polarity spell was that if it backfired, it would come back to bite us threefold. And not always in a way that could be expected.

"I need to talk with Hope about this," I said, having completely gone off the idea of breakfast. "She was weird with me last night, and now with all this… she could be going into one of her episodes."

"She's fine," Nathaniel said, waving away my concern. "She even went out for a walk this morning. I think she might finally be getting over her grief."

At this I just cocked my eyebrow and rolled my eyes. Hope hadn't gotten over Reuben since she had lost him over forty years ago. She wasn't just going to suddenly wake up one day with a mended heart.

"Where did she go?" I asked, although I already knew. She only ever went to one place on the rare occasion she would leave her tower.

"The beach," Joy added as she continued to chop and organize her various components. "Said she'd be back tonight."

"And you just let her go on her own?" I asked.

Joy gave me another reproachful expression. "She's a grown woman. And a powerful one at that, Grace. She doesn't need mollycoddling."

Although Joy and Hope were my sisters, our family situation here in the old guesthouse was more like that of a three generational family. Naturally, I was the youngest and treated as such by both of my older sisters.

Joy, being the middle one and ten years older than me, took the mother role, especially as she was effectively in charge of the Bake & Cake business. Hope, being the eldest, was the grandmother of our little set-up.

She would often treat me as the young, naive granddaughter, even though I had lived a full and varied life myself with my fair share of ups and downs, tragedies, and good experiences. But I suppose it was because none of us had children; we looked to each other to fulfill those traditional roles.

"I'm still going out to check on her," I said, grabbing some bread rolls and a flask of tea that we always made in the morning for whoever wanted to go out for a walk. Hope, however, never drank tea. There was something about the tealeaves that affected her ability.

"Don't fuss with her," Joy said. "Just let her be once you're satisfied she's okay."

"Fine, fine," I grumbled as I left the kitchen and went into the porch at the front of the old house. It was in there we kept our big coats and walking shoes. I put my favorite coat and shoes on, grabbed my walking cane, and left the house.

Noah was close by, his warm side pressing against my

leg as we headed down toward the beach. It was a nice day out, but a bit chilly.

The sun managed to peek through the ragged, grey-tinged clouds, but the cool wind blowing in off the ocean made sure that the temperatures didn't rise much beyond a few degrees above freezing.

I shivered and increased my speed in order to warm up, but when we finally reached the beach a few minutes later, a dark shape on the sand sent an icy slither up my spine.

The tide was coming in fast and had already covered the rock pools a few feet from the bundle of dark clothing. My heart seemed to stop as I raced forward. Noah went ahead of me, his nose close to the ground. When I got closer, I saw her: the still body on the sand was Hope.

Chapter Ten

At first I feared the worst. Hope wasn't moving. I knelt down beside her, reached out a hand, and gently shook her by the shoulder. Noah whined and nudged her arm with his nose.

"Hope," I said, "talk to me. Are you okay?"

My heart pounded against my chest. I looked round to see the tide coming ever closer, the white water now reaching the tips of Hope's black dress and covering

Noah's paws. With no response, I moved in closer and placed a couple of fingers on Hope's neck.

Her skin felt as cold as the wind whipping around me. Panicked, I couldn't tell if there was a pulse or not; if there was one, it had to be extremely slow. When I thought the panic would consume me, Hope's lips moved ever so slightly, parting at the middle so that her words, whatever they were, sounded like a dry whistle.

"Hope?" I said. "It's me, Grace. Can you hear me? What happened?"

Her eyes flickered open, and she stared off to the horizon and then with her strained voice said, "He's… passed on… Greg, he…"

Her words trailed off and she slumped against my arms.

Even though I was well into my fifties, I had always kept myself fit by walking and swimming—and of course, Joy's various mixes to keep me vital and young.

Hope, on the other hand, was like a tiny old bird. A small sparrow. She was easy to lift and carry away from the rising tide. With Noah woofing and staying close behind, I carried Hope across the beach until we came to the promenade that ran all the way from the Cove to Ocean View.

There was a run of benches there, and I placed Hope down on one.

Noah jumped up and lay beside her, resting his head on her legs. She moaned and held a hand to her head. Crouching in front of her to get her attention, I asked if she could hear me.

Her eyes were dark, as though her pupils had dilated to the full size of her eyes. It was quite the creepy look, but I had seen it enough times not to be too concerned.

After a few seconds of Hope staring off into who

knows where, her eyes focused on me, her pupils shrinking to normal size.

"It was him," she said, her voice croaking and barely audible over the wind as it whipped down across the promenade. A hundred meters or so to the north a young man was walking toward us. I detected his body language shift and his pace increase.

"It was who?" I asked, thinking she was referring to the man coming toward us.

"Gregory Pelt."

It fell into place then. "You mean you saw Greg's spirit pass on?"

"Isn't that what I already said? Do keep up, Grace, please."

Yup, Hope was definitely back with us, snark and all. I smiled, relieved to have my sister back to normal… well, as normal as Hope could get.

"So what made you come all the way out here?" I asked.

"I saw a vision and followed it. What else? I'm not here for the fun of it, am I?"

"No, I suppose you're not. So about Greg—did you get anything from his spirit?"

"In fact, I did," she said matter-of-factly. "You and Zach will no doubt make use of this. Greg was struck on the head by a large wrench of sorts. Something chrome or silver and heavy enough to crack his skull and kill him instantly."

"Oh," I said, taken aback by Hope's forthright sharing of information. It was normal for her to wrap up any information in some obscure game because she liked the power of having people needing her for the answers.

"Why are you just telling me this?" I asked. "Why no games?"

"Because I'm tired and I want to go home. This cold weather is going to give me hemorrhoids if I don't get back to my bed soon. Besides, Greg's spirit was in no mood for puzzles either. He wants justice, Grace, and you're the one to get it. So don't just stand there gawping at me. You've a killer to catch."

"He actually spoke to you?" I asked, surprised, as spirits usually didn't actually talk to her; there was some barrier issue or something, I had never really understood how that side of the universe worked, and frankly it scared me. I was much happier communicating with pets. You knew where you stood with them.

Spirits could be so much more… complicated.

Hope's ability to see spirits move on or just pass by was something Hope had reported a number of times over the years, so although this wasn't too surprising, it always made me shiver.

That confirmation of the whole spirit world was something I hadn't really got my head around, despite having my parents' souls inhabiting a dog and a cat.

For them, it was more of a fragment of their essence. So much so, an average person would think I was crazy for thinking my parents lived on in some capacity, but I could tell. I *knew*.

Just like Hope knew about Greg.

And now I had a lead—from the horse's mouth as it were. Now who do we know who might have access to large wrenches? A mechanic perhaps. Someone working on a car at the time of the murder? It fit nicely with my next port of call: David King's garage.

By the time Hope had fully recovered and started to complain even more about the cold weather, the man had come close enough that I recognized him.

"Dario?" I called. "Is that you?"

The man raised a hand in greeting.

I knew it was him then—Dario Donatelli from the bookstore.

He was dressed in dark walking trousers, a windproof jacket, and a wooly hat. I had never seen him wearing anything other than a finely tailored suit before, and I had to admit, I liked this new active-gent look about him.

"Good morning, ladies," he said, smiling warmly despite the redness of his cheeks beneath a frosted pair of black-rimmed spectacles. "I didn't expect to find anyone else out here at this time of day… or year."

"I'm not here out of choice," I said, giving Hope a side-eye look of displeasure. Though I couldn't be too annoyed with her; she had managed to get a clue on the case and risked hypothermia—and hemorrhoids—to do so.

"Oh?" he said, looking from Hope to me.

"Just some family stuff," I said, waving it off. "Where's Jessie?" I asked, noticing that his white Staffordshire terrier wasn't with him. Noah had seemed to notice this too, as he had gotten down from the bench and was sniffing around Dario's legs as though he could find her if he inspected hard enough.

"She's at home at the moment, curled up in her bed. She stole a piece of cake from a dinner party last night and I think it's upset her stomach, poor thing."

"Oh, I am sorry to hear that. I hope she gets better soon."

Hope rolled her eyes at me. I could tell she was about to launch into a snark-fest about dogs and how they were essentially garbage cans and could eat anything, and that we fussed too much.

Despite knowing that our father's personality was

within Noah somewhere, Hope just never took to animals the way I did.

I even felt a twinge of sadness come from Noah as he heard the news. I thought he had a crush on Jessie. But then, she was super cute, so as far as doggy-crushes went, Noah had picked a good one.

"Are we going to stand around here all day?" Hope said, deciding that the world needed to spin around her. "I do have other things to be getting on with, you know."

Sure, I thought, like sitting in your tower and scowling at the birds that came to the window for food. "Yes, Hope, we're heading back now," I said.

Dario smiled at me, seemingly finding Hope's rudeness charming. "How did you get on with the last Poirot case?" he asked me.

"Oh, I've not had a lot of time to read," I said, "things have been a little crazy lately."

"Ah, Mr. Pelt… yes, I can understand how that would make relaxing difficult."

Hope sighed with irritation and made to stand up.

Dario moved forward and offered his arm to her, which she batted away with her bony hand. She gave him a withering look that just seemed to bounce off Dario's impenetrable charm.

"I'm more than capable, young man," she said, getting to her feet and striding past me toward the way home. I let her get a few steps away and turned back to Dario.

"I'm so sorry," I said quietly. "She's having an episode. I'm sure she doesn't mean to be so rude."

"It's fine, I totally understand. I like her energy," he said.

There was something about the way he used the word *energy* that made me think he wasn't just talking about her personality.

Sure, he, like the rest of the Cove, was aware of our reputation and history, but I had the sense that he really knew something… or maybe it was just me projecting the weirdness of the morning onto a situation that had no significance.

I felt awkward and didn't respond immediately. I smiled and apologized again as Noah started to paw at Dario's jacket pocket.

"Noah!" I said. "Down, boy, don't be naughty!"

His nose was huffing and puffing and trying to get into Dario's pocket.

Dario laughed and reached out for Noah, but Noah's enthusiasm unbalanced him, sending him falling forward. Instinctively, I reached out my arms for him and took him into a hug as we both collapsed to the ground in a heap.

Noah bundled over us, licking my face and then

Dario's, then turned his attentions back to the pocket.

"What have you got in there?" I said, feeling something press against me. "Is that a banana in your pocket?"

"I say!" Hope said from somewhere behind us.

Dario managed to roll off of me and stand up. He put his hand into his pocket and pulled out a banana-shaped doggy chew.

Noah barked once and then sat still, wagging his tail, his paw up, just like he does with me when I get the treats out.

"All that for a chew?" I said, still prone.

"There's a good boy," Dario said, handing it to Noah, whose tail wagging threatened to lift him off the ground. Dario helped me up and we both dusted ourselves down.

"He's never been like that before," I said. "I'm so sorry. What have you got in that chew?" Whatever it was, Noah was crazy for it. I was getting a sense of him being in some kind of doggy nirvana.

"An old family recipe," he said with that charming grin of his. "I always carry them for Jessie."

"Ah, that explains it," I said. "Noah's got a crush on Jessie and must have picked up on her scent."

"Honestly," Hope said, her bony arms on her hips. "You two are carrying on like teenagers. I'll see you at home, Grace." Shaking her head, and with her strength clearly gathered, she strode off up the hill toward home, leaving us alone.

Feeling super awkward from the fall and Hope's outburst, I sat on the bench to recover.

Dario joined me, and Noah lay at our feet, enjoying his new chew treat.

In a wave of emotion, I slumped forward, putting my head in my hands. I felt weak, embarrassed, and overwhelmed all at once. I felt exhausted. Finding Hope lying on the beach like that and then getting the revelation from her just drained me for a moment.

"What is it, Grace? Are you okay?"

Taking a deep breath, I sat back up and nodded. "I will be, Dario. I'm sorry about all this. I'm not normally this… I don't even know what the word is. Things are just really odd at the moment."

"It's understandable," he said, his voice reverberating with that wonderful baritone sound of his. I turned to look at him. He had taken his glasses off and I could see his eyes, large and brown, and although a complete cliché, I felt myself swimming in them.

He inched closer to me. I could feel the heat of his face on mine.

"You've had a lot of stress lately," he said.

I nodded, his words kind of echoing around in my

head, soothing away my anxiety and embarrassment. "I have."

"And it's okay to feel a bit strained. But you're strong, and you will figure things out. Have faith in your skills, Grace. But beware false prophets."

Before I had a chance to ask what he meant, glorious warmth gathered around me and I seemed to shift away into a kind of sleep. A sleep that my mind and body gladly reached out and took.

I was no longer on the promenade bench, below the lights, out there in the cold. I was somewhere warm, featureless, and calming.

And then I was nowhere at all.

Chapter Eleven

It was the craziest thing. Somehow, when I had come around from that warm, comforting darkness, I opened my eyes and found myself standing outside the Guesthouse with Noah by my side.

I'd experienced plenty of weird things in my life, but how I managed to walk all the way home with no recollection at all was ranked high on the weird-o-meter.

To add to the general weirdness, I didn't even really

care. In fact, I felt amazing.

It was as though someone had just told me I had won the lottery, or I had found a ticket for a trip on the Orient Express. The smile on my face must have made me look a little silly, but the feel-good vibes warming me from my toes to my scalp meant I didn't care.

"Don't suppose you can tell me what happened?" I asked Noah, who just looked up at me with those soulful eyes of his, no answers to be found.

But I did get a memory: Noah chewing the treat he had got from Dario, then sitting on the bench, staring into Dario's…

That was it!

The old rogue must have hypnotized me or something.

As soon as that thought came into my head, I was compelled to fumble a hand into my coat pocket. I pulled out a small piece of yellow paper with Dario's bookstore letterhead logo embossed on the top.

Beneath that was a neatly handwritten note that simply said: *Call me sometime.* And below that a phone number I assumed was his personal number, as it was different to the store's.

Now, I didn't think that being hypnotized without one's agreement was polite or even welcomed, but given how I was feeling at the time and how I felt when I returned home, I had to agree that Dario did the right thing.

We were old friends and I knew he wouldn't have done it maliciously. He was just looking out for me. And, even more importantly, by doing this, he had not so subtly revealed to me that he was more than just a suave, charming bookstore owner.

What he actually was, however, still wasn't entirely clear at that point.

I made a note to call him later that day to set up a date where I could investigate further.

The thought of that only added to my enthusiasm and well-being, and I opened the door and headed toward the kitchen, deciding to have a cup of tea before heading back out again.

"Where've you been?" Joy asked as soon as I stepped through to the kitchen.

She wore a worried expression as she stood behind one of the kitchen islands with her arms crossed firmly. "Hope's been back for ages and said you would be right behind her."

Joy glared at me for a moment before turning her head to regard Nathaniel, who was talking in an animated fashion to a man wearing a shiny, cheap-looking suit.

"I decided to take a bit of a walk on the promenade," I said. It wasn't entirely a lie.

Although I didn't like to hold anything back from my family, until I knew exactly what Dario was up to, I didn't want to cause any undue worry for Joy, as she had had enough of that over the last few days.

I gestured to the man and raised an eyebrow.

He was smiling widely at Nathaniel in the predatory way a used-car salesman would. He had a close-shaved head and a small beard on the tip of his chin. I didn't need to access Noah's canine sense of smell to 'experience' the pungent effect of the man's terrible cologne.

Despite not hearing what he and Nathaniel were talking about, the fact they were at the far end of the kitchen and standing in front of the 'murder oven' told me it was about a likely replacement.

I stepped closer to the kitchen island and noticed Joy was rolling out some pastry. She had a number of shaped cutters and varied bowls of dried fruit arranged around her rolling area.

"Looks nice," I said. "What are you making?"

"Some fruit rolls, a new recipe," Joy said.

"So that must mean you're more confident of meeting the deadline for the banquet?"

It was always a good sign to see Joy cooking and baking. It was like watching a lion in the wild; it just made sense. She was born for it.

Dropping her voice a little and leaning closer, Joy said, "He's a kitchen appliance salesman. Says he's interested in taking our old oven in part exchange for a new one. Nathaniel is negotiating the best price."

"Where's this guy from?"

"It's the craziest of things," Joy said, smiling with just a hint of guilt at the edges of her eyes. "He was just passing through town, on his way to some big stove and kitchen expo in Salem, when he heard about our predicament."

Hmm, I thought. It was quite the coincidence. Something that wouldn't normally happen unless there was something else prompting this piece of good fortune.

"It was Mum's recipe that did this, wasn't it?" I said.

"Oh, I don't know," Joy said, focusing on her pastry now. "It could just be a natural coincidence. One must not look a gift horse in the mouth when in a desperate situation."

One didn't need the deductive powers of Sherlock Holmes to know this salesman was not here because of anything natural. This was Mum's magic, and there was no denying it. I could sense the ephemeral energies in the kitchen.

The small hairs on the back of my neck tingled as though someone had opened a door from somewhere in the house, only it was less of a cold tingle and more of a static electrical tingle—one we Angelos had come to know very well.

It was the sensation of powerful magic at play.

The salesman seemed to have finally realized I was in the room, spun round, smiled even wider so that he appeared like a snake getting ready to devour something much larger than himself, and approached me.

He thrust his bony hand out. “Charlie Carnegie, at your service Ms…?”

“Grace Angelo,” I said, taking his hand, and shrinking away almost immediately in reaction to his cold, clammy touch. I didn't want to say it was a pleasure to meet him, because frankly it wasn't.

My aversion had no effect on his confidence, though, as he explained the deal so far.

“So, I've just been chatting with your family about your… unfortunate situation with your oven here. It's a fine unit. They don't make them like that anymore. It's such a shame… such a shame."

He fidgeted in his cheap suit and kept running one hand down his left lapel. The kitchen lights reflected off his shiny face, and I imagined it would feel as clammy as his hands.

"He wants to charge us a removal fee," Nathaniel said, joining us by the kitchen island.

"It's a health issue," Carnegie said. "Not a cheap procedure. There's paperwork that needs completing, red tape, you know the kind of thing. It all slices into the bottom line."

"Why do you even want it?" I asked. "You do understand that there was a dead person in there not so long ago?"

He shrugged as though it were no big deal. "It's been cleared by the police. A quick clean-up and a service and it'll be fine to use. Those big industrial units don't come onto the used market very often."

"So what is a replacement and the removal fee going to cost us?" Joy asked.

"Well, madam, as I was explaining to your good husband, there's a lot of things to consider with a deal like this..." On and on he went, quoting various laws and regulations and associated costs.

In the end, Nathaniel had clearly had enough and blurted out, "It's going to cost four thousand dollars if we want the new oven installed this afternoon."

Joy's eyebrows shot up. "Four thousand! We don't have that kind of money. You said this was valuable to you and would do us a good part-exchange deal."

"I've already waived the handling fee and extraction costs, madam. It's also not easy to have a new one shipped and installed in the same day. My contractors are busy people. I'd have to take them off another job, and that requires compensation."

"Is that really the best price you can do?" I asked. "What if we were to help your contractors with the removal and fitting? Nathaniel is a very capable handyman."

Carnegie smiled at me again as though I were a mouse about to be devoured. I was really starting to dislike this guy. "I'm sorry, it's against county law to have non-registered contractors work on gas appliances. No insurance company would cover it if there were to be an accident. And I'm sure you wouldn't want that, would you?"

As we continued to negotiate back and forth, Joy wandered over to the far side of the kitchen and reached up into her special cupboard where she kept some of her more powerful spell components.

She pulled out an old, dusty tea caddie and levered the top off with a butter knife. Then, looking over her shoulder, she said, "Mr. Carnegie, why don't you join us for a cup of tea. I'm sure we could do with a short break before we agree to your deal and fill out all the paperwork."

"That would be wonderful, thank you," Carnegie said. "I am quite parched now that you come to mention it."

"Please go through to the parlor, I'll bring the tea through shortly. Show him the way, won't you, Nate?"

Nathaniel did just that, leaving me in the kitchen alone with Joy—and Noah, who had remained sitting by the island, chewing the remnants of the treat Dario had given to him.

"Joy," I said as I joined her at the counter, "you're not doing what I think you're doing, are you?"

"I don't know what you're thinking, sis."

I stepped closer and peered inside the tea caddy. The smell was pungent and clung to the back of my throat like sulfur. Diabolical indeed. Joy fished around inside and pulled out an old teabag that appeared to have some kind of mold growing on it.

Guiltily, Joy looked up at me, but there was more than just guilt in her eyes—she had a tired, almost desperate look to her.

"Joy? What are you planning to do?"

She closed her eyes and sighed, then shook her head. "Oh, I don't know anymore," she said. "This whole business with poor Greg and the banquet has really got me on edge. I know I'm not making rational choices, but really, what choice do we have?"

"What's in that teabag?"

At first she didn't say anything, just stared at the old moldy object, and then, resigned to the fact I wasn't going to let it go, said, “It's a compulsion component. It'll make Mr. Carnegie more susceptible. More… agreeable.”

I peered over my shoulder to make sure we were alone and then turned back to Joy. “We can't do that, not like this. Things are already strange as it is. That good fortune spell has brought Mr. Carnegie to us; we can't push our luck. Who knows what the cost will really be?”

“I just don't see any other option. We don't have that kind of money, and if we lose that contract, we'll be in a worse situation yet. This place is falling down around our ears, and Nathaniel is at the stretching point with what he can do with the repairs. I'm desperate, Grace. I don't know what to do anymore.”

She dropped the tea bag back into the caddy and let out a sob. I grabbed her into a hug and told her it would be okay. “Listen, I've got a plan. Just promise me you won't resort to this kind of magic. It's too uncertain.”

"But how are we going to get out of this?" she said, choking back her tears.

"Leave it to me. You trust me, don't you?"

"Then tell me what you have planned."

Before I could explain, Mr. Carnegie appeared in the doorway. "Are you two ladies okay?" he said. Nathaniel soon appeared behind him, looking concerned.

"We're fine," I said. "Please, take a seat. We'll be right with you." I gave Nathaniel a knowing look that told him to trust me.

Once everyone had calmed down and took their seats in the parlor, leaving me alone in the kitchen, I sat down on one of the stools and considered my plan.

I had always hoped things wouldn't come to this.

As if knowing what I was planning, Charity leapt out of nowhere and landed on the kitchen island, right in front of my face. Her piercing eyes stared into mine, and

I felt a wave of disappointment hit me.

"I'm sorry," I said quietly to Charity, knowing I was going beyond the cat part of her soul and reaching directly to the spirit of my mother. "It's the only way. The amulet is the only thing valuable enough to get us out of this situation."

The amulet, being the only physical thing I had from my mother, was more valuable to me than just the financial value, but we really had no other way out.

Our credit rating with the bank was so low they wouldn't extend our overdraft.

We had piled all our remaining savings into the upkeep of the Guesthouse and the setting up of the Cake & Bake, and that only made a modest profit—enough for us to keep trading and get by.

"Joy's not exaggerating that this could ruin us," I said to my mother's spirit.

Charity flicked her tail angrily and reached her paw up for the amulet.

I received a flash of an image that I couldn't quite make out—a blinding white blanket of light and then, in the middle, a silhouette started to emerge, then it dissipated, to be replaced with an image of the old tea caddy.

"No," I said. "We're not using your old magic. You know better than us what that can do!"

Charity meowed at me sharply and scratched my hand with her claws before darting off somewhere into the house.

Noah pressed against my leg and huffed sadly. I reached down and ran my hand through his soft, warm fur. "I'm sorry, Father," I said. "I know you understand why I have to do this."

He rubbed his snout against my hand in sympathy.

Although his love for my mother was unbreakable, he always knew that she was impetuous, even dangerous at times. I knew that a certain amount of that personality had found its way into Joy, which was why I was so strict with her.

We had to use our powers responsibly; otherwise, we'd end up like Hope and our mother, and that was a fate neither of us would want.

I came to terms with the fact that I would have to mend bridges with Charity/my mother after pawning the amulet, and come up with a plan to get it back, but for now, I needed to deal with Carnegie and make sure we had an oven in place to meet our contract.

I went into the parlor and held out my hand to Mr. Carnegie. "Sir, you have a deal," I said. "I'll pay your fee in total this evening upon installation of the new oven. I'm afraid I can't pay you now, as I need to go into town to arrange the money. I hope this is acceptable, as it's the only deal we can agree to."

Carnegie nearly snapped my hand off my wrist. "Deal!" he said. "I'll have my men get to work right away. If you would just sign this bill of sale, we can conclude this and have your business back up and running as quickly as possible."

Joy wouldn't look at me during this entire exchange. I left Nathaniel to deal with the paperwork and left to get back on with the case. I needed to get out of the house anyway and clear my head. On my way to David King's I'd drop in at the pawn shop and raise the money needed.

"I'll be back later this evening," I said from the front porch.

Only Nathaniel replied.

There was no sign of Charity, but Noah was right there, my shadow.

"You're such a sweet man," I said to him, kissing him on the head. "Let's go do some sleuthing and see if we can find this wrench."

He licked my face and darted out of the house. I grabbed my hiking stick and strode after him, happy to be moving again, even if it was in the cold, chilly December air.

Before I headed to King's garage, though, I made a beeline toward the high street. I just wanted to get this whole amulet business over and done with. The quicker I pawned it and paid Carnegie, the quicker I could work out a plan to buy it back.

The fee I usually get from the police for being a consultant would only make a small dent, so I'd need to figure something else out.

But before that, I had David King to contend with.

Chapter Twelve

The main street was busy with tourists and townsfolk. They filled the sidewalks with a buzz of energy that always came around on the month leading to Christmas. I had to grip extra hard on my walking cane to make sure I wasn't bundled over.

With the cold wind whipping at my face, I was relieved to get inside Patty's Pawnshop. The decor hadn't changed in nearly a hundred years.

The walls were dark wood and were covered in dust and grime that held all kinds of wild stories. For many years before Patty and her family bought the place, it had served as one of the first trading posts.

And by trading post, I mean smuggling den.

Sagging shelves covered the walls on both sides, leaving a central space through the shop that led to the old counter. The worn wooden top sat above a glass cabinet filled with various curios and valuable items.

The only thing that spoke of modernity was the laptop on the counter and the blinking red LED security light inside of the cabinet that I guessed was hooked up to an alarm, giving the expensiveness of some of the items within.

Noah huffed with a doggy sneeze, and my own nose twitched as dust filled the air.

Behind the laptop stood Patty's son, Tony-Joe, known

to everyone as TJ.

He was in his mid-sixties and had recently taken over the running of the shop full time, as Patty was getting a little too old to run the place. And by her definition of 'too old', that meant ninety-three.

Whatever Patty did with her life had worked. Even in her nineties, she had proved to be a shrewd and capable businesswoman. I was glad in some ways that it was TJ behind the counter. He hadn't yet earned Patty's reputation of a fierce negotiator.

"Hey, Grace, Noah, nice to see you both today. Cold out this time of year, ain't it?"

A mirror behind him, in an antique gold frame, showed a reflection of my face. Through the covering dust I saw how red my skin was, the chilled air doing its best to ruin my attempts to moisturize.

"Sure is, TJ."

"We recently got in some ski masks from those posh people up at Ocean View. Perhaps I could recommend one for you to help keep the cold off your beautiful face?"

TJ's floppy brown hair jiggled around his square, bearded chin and shoulders as he smiled. His terrible attempt at salesmanship... and flirting, I supposed, made him appear much younger than his years, despite the old-fashioned brown pinstriped suit he wore.

Patty hadn't really let him out into the world much, so everything with him just felt a little off, although he wasn't lacking in sincerity.

I smiled at the icebreaker and stepped up to the counter. Noah brushed against my legs and wandered off around the shop. It must have been hurting him to see me pawning the amulet, but I appreciated the lack of hostility about it.

If only Charity could have seen it the same way.

“I'll get straight to the point,” I said, pulling the amulet out of my pocket and placing it carefully on a leather blotter on the countertop. “This has been in my family for many generations and is quite valuable. Well, more than 'quite', I'm sure you realize. I'm not looking to pawn it for a Patty price either. Give me a fair evaluation and we can do a deal.”

“Okay,” TJ said, raising his thick brown eyebrows as he focused on the amulet.

The emerald stone set within the gold oval always grabbed people's attention.

“I'll need a few minutes to value it properly. Do you mind if I take this out back and look up the particulars?” TJ pointed to an open doorway. Inside was another old, battered wooden desk. On a shelf above it were many leather-bound books that I had seen Patty poring over throughout the years. They were catalogues and indexes for valuing items.

"You won't find it in any of your books," I said. "It's a custom piece. The maker died nearly a century ago now."

"That's very useful, thanks," he said. "I can still use the catalogues to get a rough idea of the materials' worth. If that's okay?"

"Sure, go ahead," I said, ignoring the pounding heart in my chest as TJ carefully and respectfully lifted the amulet up and took it through to the other room and placed it with reverence on a soft cloth atop the desk.

While TJ was doing his research, I received a text from Zach. It said that Suzanne Manning's alibi checked out, that the video footage did, in fact, prove that she was in the diner all night, talking with her daughter. I sent a message back to tell him I was on my way to David King's and would let him know the outcome.

I wished I had him here with me instead of his being

in Salem.

My heart was still beating hard, and my hands became clammy.

Just as I was about to lean over the counter and ask TJ if he was finished yet, he appeared in the doorway and took his position behind the laptop, placing the amulet back on the counter.

“It really is a beautiful piece,” he said. “I'm just going to verify something on the Net...” His attention drifted down to the laptop screen. He tapped a few things in and then used his mouse once and then twice, then, looking at it with an expression of annoyance on his face, shook it.

“Damn thing's stopped working again,” he said. “I only replaced the batteries a few hours ago. That's the third set in the last couple of days.”

“Must be something in the air,” I said. “My watch

battery died on me a few days ago."

"They just don't make things like they used to, do they?" TJ said and returned to the keyboard.

I just smiled and waited.

Noah returned to me and sat against my leg, his warmth helping to calm me.

"So," TJ eventually said, "I think the best I can offer for you this is four and half thousand."

"But the last evaluation we had on it was nearly twice that," I said. I wasn't lying either. We had it evaluated a few years prior for insurance.

TJ gave me a sympathetic look and raised his shoulders. "I'm sorry, but that's the best we can do. We can't risk the full worth. This is just a small town, after all. For us, this is quite the large investment, and we don't hold that much cash on the premises."

We negotiated back and forth for a few minutes, but it

didn't help.

TJ genuinely was offering his best deal. Noah had picked up on his sincerity and let me know in that weird, fuzzy brain communication thing of his.

Still, even though it wasn't its full worth, it was enough to pay Mr. Carnegie with a little left over to get the supplies we needed to make the products for the banquet.

Reluctantly, I reached my hand over the countertop and said, "You've got a deal."

My guts churned as TJ handed me the money and the receipt. He locked the amulet inside the glass cabinet and ensured me it would be secure. I had seven days to buy it back and then it would be up for general sale.

When we left the shop, I had a tear in my eye, but also a feeling of hope that I had at least raised the money for the new oven.

Before I went over to question David King, I visited the bank and deposited the money, and at the same time I got a cashier's check to give to Mr. Carnegie.

That way, I wouldn't have to feel so vulnerable walking around with four and half thousand dollars in my jacket pocket. With that task done, I was actually looking forward to getting back to the case. I wasn't good at all this emotional family stuff. I missed the thrill of the investigation.

*

King's garage was a thirty-minute walk out of town.

By the time I got there, it was just after noon and David was opening up again after his lunch break. He saw me walking up the gravel path and raised a hand in greeting.

David King looked just like Tom Hanks, which I had always found entertaining. He even had a slight twang to his accent that made me think of Forrest Gump. Today, he was wearing his hair closely cropped. He wore a red flannel shirt beneath his dirty grey-blue coveralls.

"Afternoon, Grace," he said a little cautiously as he squinted against the sun that was at my back. "I guess this is about my pa?"

"Actually, it's about you and Michelle Dechamps that I've come to talk to you about. Is your father still upset about my questioning?"

"Yep," David said. He turned his back and entered the garage. "You better come on back," he said over his shoulder.

Noah and I followed inside. The place was surprisingly warm, even with the large garage doors open. Taking up the central work place was Michelle Dechamps's red convertible Mustang.

I was no car nut, but I had to say I understood the fascination. It was a beautiful machine, only marred by the right front fender that wasn't shiny red like the rest of the body. David poked his head out of a small office at the back of the garage. "Can I get you some tea?" he asked.

"No, thanks, I'm in a bit of a rush, actually."

He stepped out and joined me at the front of the Mustang.

"What happened to it?" I said, noting the grey primer on the fender.

"Michelle had a little… um, incident."

I raised an eyebrow at the same time Noah nudged me a little. That was his way of telling me that there was something else behind that.

"Michelle told me you were just doing some work on it

because she had recently bought it from a guy in the Hamptons. She didn't mention she had had an accident."

David stepped from one foot to the other and wrung an old rag between his hands. He wouldn't look me in the eye, preferring to keep his gaze on the car instead.

"David," I said, sterner now, "what happened here, and please, let me remind you I'm here on official business at Zachary's request. I could escalate this if you don't tell me the truth."

It took a few moments, but David seemed to realize that I had caught on to something. He was a fairly honest character, despite being one of the Kings, and I could tell something was troubling him.

I placed a hand on his shoulder until he looked up at me.

"Listen, we don't have to let this go to Zachary, if you're just honest with me."

"Fine, fine," he said, shaking his head. "Michelle's already put me in a difficult situation. It ain't my fault she's hiding this. Besides, my pa and I weren't getting paid any more for this work that night. You should have heard when she came over, ordering us around as though we were her private slaves or something. I had to hold Pops back…"

He trailed off, realizing what I had just spotted.

"You're saying that on the night of Greg's murder, your father was here helping you work on the car?"

Without saying a word, he just nodded. I could see the tension on his face.

"You do know," I said, "that your father told me he was with your mother all night. You just contradicted his alibi. Now why would he lie about being here with you?"

David didn't say anything, but Noah tapped his snout against my leg to get my attention.

I looked down at him and saw that he was staring up into the far right corner of the garage.

There, in the corner, was a security camera.

David saw that I saw this and his face went pale.

"You have tapes for that, I assume," I said. "I can get a warrant for you to provide those as evidence. If your father was here, we'll know, and it would prove that he lied to us. That won't look good for either of you."

"But it also proves we didn't have anything to do with Greg," he said. "We were here all night. Pops came here right after being thrown out of the bar and helped me work on the fender."

"So why the lie? What are you two hiding from me? You know this can get difficult for you if I escalate this with Zachary and the DA's office, David. It's best if you're honest with me. I am on your side."

He took a deep breath, sighed and agreed. "Okay," he

said, “I'll tell you. It would come out eventually I'm sure anyway.”

“Go on,” I prompted.

“Michelle didn't hit the tree through an accident as such. See, she tried to hit Casey Foster, for having an affair with Greg. Only she missed and careened into a tree. To avoid the insurance and having it come out what she was planning to do, she came to Pops and me to fix the car so it looked like there was no accident. Pops also took care of the tree so there was no evidence.”

“So you're saying that you and your father helped cover up an attempted murder?”

“No! No, nothing like that, really. She wasn't going to kill her, just trying to scare her, but she lost control and hit the tree. Casey didn't even know it was her; she was too busy listening to her music, and Michelle managed to drive away before she was spotted. It was all just a stupid accident. No one got hurt."

"Well, I'm not sure about that," I said. "Greg was killed after all."

"But it was none of us, we were all here. I'll even give you the video from the security camera to prove it. Pops was only lying to protect Michelle's story. You've got to believe me, I had nothing to do with this."

I did believe him, but I insisted on him handing over the video files. While he was busying himself in the office to arrange that, I snooped about the garage to find anything that could qualify as a large wrench. With Noah's help, we covered every inch of the garage, including all the toolboxes and shelves, and found nothing larger than a regular socket wrench, which wasn't at all the kind of thing Hope had communicated with me.

When David came out, I asked him outright, "Do you

have any large wrenches here?" I showed him with my hands the size I was referring to.

He scrunched his face as he thought about it and shook his head. "Nothing that big," he said. "Just regular tools. I have a few lever bars used for jacks, but they're just straight bars, not wrenches. Why do you ask?"

"Oh, no reason," I said. "Just wondering out loud."

"For wrenches that large," he said as he handed me a bundle of USB sticks, "you'll probably be looking at some kind of heavy machinery shop. There's one on the other side of town that works on farming machinery. If not, you'll be able to hire one at the tool hire in the next town."

"That's useful to know, thanks, David. I best be off, then. Thanks for helping me out."

"You're not going to tell Michelle it was me that spilled the truth about her accident, are you?"

“I can't promise that,” I said. “I'll need to speak with Zachary first and see what he wants to do, but if your video does confirm what you say, you can at least rest easy knowing you and your father will be eliminated from the murder investigation.”

Before I left, David said, “I hope you find the person who did that to Greg. I know most of my family didn't get on with him, and that he was a cheat, but really, he wasn't a terrible person. We got on quite well, in fact. I've known people far worse than him. He didn't deserve this.”

“I know,” I said, feeling David's sincerity wash off him. “I'll do my best.”

With that, I headed back home, eager to get the oven situation sorted out once and for all. I also had to call Zach about what I had found out, and lastly… call Dario.

We had a lot to talk about.

Chapter Thirteen

I arrived home to find a large U-Haul truck out front. A couple of equally large men were wrestling the old 'murder oven' into the back of it. Carnegie was standing at the door, chatting with Nathaniel. Both men turned and smiled at me as I approached.

"Grace, you're back," Nathaniel said with a strained smile and expectation in his eyes. I could tell he was eager to get rid of the salesman, who kind of lurked there in the shadows, waiting like some kind of spider.

He too looked at me with expectation with those beady eyes of his. I shivered and avoided his gaze. "Mr. Carnegie," I said, handing him the cashier's check. "I believe this is all in order."

The salesman snatched it from my hand faster than Noah snatching a doggy bake. He held it up to the late afternoon sun as though he was checking if it were a fake.

"It's real," I said with a sharp snap. "I can assure you of that. If you're in any doubt, I'd be happy to wait for you to call the bank."

"Oh no, no, that's fine, Ms. Angelo. I'm more than happy and trust you implicitly," Carnegie said, tucking the now folded check into the top breast pocket of his white shirt. "Well, that concludes our business," he added, not even offering to shake our hands as he strode to the truck. “Happy baking!”

With that, he got into the passenger side and waited for his two workmen to join him. In a few seconds, the truck reversed out of the drive and headed up the winding road toward the center of town.

I exhaled at the same time as Nathaniel.

“I'm so glad it's all over,” I said.

“Me too! Grace, we can't thank you enough for what you've done. I promise you, we'll do our best to raise the funds and get your amulet back as quick as we possibly can. I know how much it means to you.”

“It's what family is for, brother-in-law.”

Nathaniel hugged me and kissed me on the cheek. “You're the best, sister-in-law. Okay, let's get you inside where it's warm. Joy has someone she wants you to meet.”

The smell of baking hit me as soon as I entered the

house. It brought a wide smile to my face and a growl to my belly. The scent of baking cinnamon always did that. Joy was a true master of pastries. She was the first to see me as I walked into the kitchen, Noah by my side.

"Grace! I can't thank you enough. Carnegie was good for his word. The new oven is fantastic, even better than our old one. I really think we're going to meet the deadline now… oh, that reminds me, look who came to help us."

A young girl with long curly brown hair and piercing green eyes smiled at me. "Hello, Aunty Grace. Remember me?"

"Kendra! How could I forget a face like that?"

"I would hug you, but… um, there was an accident with the flour…"

Kendra smiled, flashing her beautifully straight white teeth.

She was the picture of my mother when she was in her early twenties. The similarity threw me for a moment, the whole amulet thing finally hitting me, but I managed to compose myself and welcome Kendra to our home. She was Joy and Nathaniel's god-daughter. I hadn't seen her since she was just twelve years old, over a decade ago.

We briefly caught up, and Kendra told me that she was studying metallurgy at college and wanted to be an engineer when she graduated. I was tempted to ask her if she'd like to get some work experience by helping Nathaniel with the repairs to the Guesthouse, but I resisted.

"Charity around?" I asked.

Joy looked down at the floor and shook her head. There was an unspoken regret on both our parts. I knew it would take a while for her to forgive me for pawning the amulet she had handed down to me.

Still, it was done now and I had to focus on the future. I excused myself and went up to my room. Noah followed and flopped down at the foot of my bed on the pile of blankets that made up his favorite sleeping place.

As I was getting changed out of my cold, damp clothes, I noticed the piece of paper from Dario. Wanting to get that small mystery dealt with, I grabbed my cell and called the number.

He answered on the third ring.

"Grace," he said with a kind, happy voice. "So glad to hear from you. I trust you got home okay?"

"You know I did," I said, with a little more aggression than I intended. "I'm sorry, I didn't mean it to sound like that, but we do need to talk… about what you did. And why. Can we meet for a meal tonight? I really could do with a nice meal and a bottle of wine."

"That's just what I had in mind too," he said.

"Wait, you didn't implant this thought into me, did you?"

He chuckled warmly, and despite myself, I smiled. "Nothing of the sort, Grace. I would never do anything like that to you. But yes, I would very much like to meet with you this evening. I know I have some explaining to do, and I would rather do that face to face than over the phone."

"The meal is on you, though," I said. "I've had some rather unexpected costs to cover lately. And after your little stunt, you do kind of owe me."

That warm chuckle came over the line again, making me smile. Feel-good vibes travelled all through my body, and I couldn't tell if it was just the excitement of the date or whether he was doing something with his abilities.

"I heard about the whole oven issue," he said. "I dropped in earlier and spoke with Nate. You did a good thing, Grace. You saved your family business. So, yes, it would be an honor to buy you dinner. Shall we say 8:00 p.m? I can come and pick you up."

"Where were you thinking of taking me?"

There was a brief pause before he said, "How does the Pumpkin Parlor sound?"

Despite its name, the 'Double P', as it was known in town, was actually a very high-class restaurant, usually only frequented by those wealthy types from the Ocean View community. I had only been there once for a charity event, but the experience had stayed with me. It was an amazing place.

"Grace? Are you still there?" Dario asked.

"Um, yeah, sorry, I was just… never mind, the Double P would be just perfect."

"Great, I'll come by at eight. I'll see you then."

"Thanks, Dario. I'll see you tonight."

We said our goodbyes and the call was done. I sat down on the edge of the bed and exhaled a breath I hadn't realized I was holding. Noah looked up at me with expectation.

"I'm sorry, Noah, I can't take you with me. They don't allow dogs into the restaurant."

He whined a little, reminding me he was no normal dog.

"I know, but they don't know that," I said. "How about I bring you home a doggy bag courtesy of Dario?"

Woof!

Noah sat up and placed his head on my lap. I scratched his ears and kissed him on the head. "You're such a sweet thing. I just wish Charity could be as understanding as you."

A text notification on my cell interrupted that line of inquiry.

It was from Zach telling me that the tech guys up at Salem had said that the image Francesca had provided as her alibi checked out.

I replied, thanking him for letting me know, and also added what I had learned from David King. This reminded me about the USB sticks. For the next few hours while I waited to get ready for the meal with Dario, I watched the video footage on my laptop, and nothing at all seemed out of the ordinary.

It showed exactly what David had said it would: Callum and Michelle turning up at the times they were supposed to, and the two Kings working on the car. I briefly called Zach to let him know, but he didn't answer, so I left a message on his voicemail.

I sighed with frustration and threw my cell phone onto the bed.

"This investigation just keeps hitting dead ends," I said

to Noah, wincing at my own inappropriate pun.

His bushy eyebrows twitched as he picked up my cell in his mouth and brought it to me. I took it from him. "What is it?"

He woofed and nudged his snout against the phone again.

I looked down at the screen. It was the image Francesca had sent. "It checks out," I said. "Zach had his technical buddies check it out."

I got a wave of urgency from Noah as though there was still something wrong with it. I looked again at the picture and couldn't work out what he was getting at. It showed Francesca and Abe together, a clock in the background. In the top right corner a slither of a TV showed. On the other side, there was a glow on the curtains from a lamp.

"What is it?" I asked Noah again. "I'm not seeing

anything."

Noah lay down on his paws and huffed.

Shrugging my shoulders, I placed the cell on my dresser and continued to get ready for my date. Dario would be picking me up in less than an hour. "I don't know what you've seen," I said as I put on a little makeup. "If you've got any answers, I'd be happy to hear them."

Noah just whined softly and curled up in his blankets.

Within minutes, he was snoozing with a wheezing kind of snore that told me he would be out for the count for many hours to come. It had been a tiring day, after all, so I couldn't blame him. For a moment I felt like calling Dario to tell him I was too tired for the date, but deep down I knew I needed the break.

And then there was the whole mystery of what Dario actually was.

It wasn't unheard of to have male witches in Hemlock

Cove, but the last one I had heard about had died over fifty years ago, and he had only lived in the Cove for a short while before going back to his native Boston.

I sat there at my dresser, fixing my hair and making sure I looked respectable when I saw the yellow lights of Dario's car slice through the darkness outside of my window.

My room overlooked the front of the house. I approached the window and saw his old classic black Maserati pull up outside.

Dario stepped out, dressed impeccably, as he always was. This time he wore a gorgeous fitted slate-blue suit. He walked up to the door and rang the bell.

Even though I watched it happen, it still made me jump, and my stomach fluttered a little with butterflies. It had been so long since I had been on a date, I felt like a schoolgirl again getting ready for her prom.

Despite my excitement, my thoughts went to my late husband. I knew his spirit was out there somewhere looking down on me. I felt no animosity or fear, which told me he approved.

"It's just to find out who he is and what he did," I said quietly to the memory of my dear Samson. Warmth wrapped around my body, telling me it was okay.

With Noah still snoozing and Charity still missing, I grabbed my little black clutch bag, placed my cell inside, and headed downstairs in my black dress and heels to meet my charming date for the evening.

Chapter Fourteen

The Pumpkin Parlor was as spectacular as I remembered it.

Despite wearing my swankiest dress, and getting a surprising amount of attention from the male fraternity within the restaurant, I still felt entirely out of place.

Sitting opposite me, Dario looked every inch *in place.* Suave was just the first word that came to mind, quickly followed by charming, handsome, and most of all—kind.

"This food is amazing," I said. I forked another piece of my grilled vegetable gratin and slowly devoured the amazing flavors. "How's your lasagna?"

"It's great," Dario said. "Though somewhat put into the shadows by the excellent company. You really do look beautiful, Grace. I don't think I ever really made it obvious, but I've had a crush on you for the best part of a decade."

"Oh, you're making me blush. Stop it!" I said, though I didn't really want him to stop. It had been such a long time since anyone had taken me out and really treated me well. It reminded me of the many nights Samson and I shared together.

I was worried that I would feel awkward; since Samson had been gone, I'd kind of kept myself out of this whole romance side of life, even though I knew, somehow, that Samson would be happy for me, I just hadn't up until now been able to feel comfortable with it myself.

But I suppose because Dario had been a good platonic friend for so many years, it made the whole thing much easier. I didn't doubt his intentions and I trusted him, which for me was the most important thing.

However, there was still the issue of the hypnotism or whatever it was that he did to me.

I waited until the skilled waiting staff took away our plates and brought us our desserts to finally raise the question. By this time, I had drunk three glasses of wine and felt a bit more assertive about the whole situation.

"So, Dario, about this morning on the promenade," I began. "You want to tell me what was up with that?" I smiled before taking a spoonful of the amazing pumpkin cheesecake—one of the restaurants most famed dishes.

"I guess I do owe you an explanation," Dario said. He had ordered an orange sorbet, and like my dessert, it looked amazing. But then for the prices, it had to be. This was by far the most expensive meal I had ever had.

I waited for him to finish his dessert and prompted him again after the waiting staff had removed our plates. There was nothing between us now and we both leaned in like conspirators, or lovers… but I didn't want to think too much about that.

Dario looked around the dimly lit restaurant as though he were worried someone was spying on him, but the fifty or so patrons were too busy in their booths and at their tables, enjoying romantic moments or what looked like varied business discussions.

"Okay," he finally said, dabbing at the corners of his mouth with his napkin. "I come from a long lineage that traces its roots back to pre-Christian times. My family came from a Mediterranean tribe of… there isn't really a modern word for them, but we've been called warlocks and wizards throughout the ages, though that's really not very accurate at all."

"So you know about…"

"Magic? Your family, that you're a… witch?" he said this in such hushed tones I could only just make out what he said. "Yes, I know all about that. My people, we… it's hard to explain, and it's a little crowded here to go into details. Why don't we go somewhere a little more private?"

"Oh? I didn't think you would be this forward, Mr. Donatelli," I said with a smirk.

He returned a charming smile and I saw the smallest hint of a blush to his cheeks. "You know what I mean, Grace. Look, it's exceptionally warm for this time of year, how about we take a walk on the beach? It is only five minutes from here, after all."

Eager to know more, I agreed. Dario paid the bill, which was super kind of him, and we took a five-minute drive to the small parking lot on the promenade.

He was right; it was quite warm out for a mid-December evening, but I also suspected it wasn't entirely natural. As we walked along the beach in bare feet, he continued to tell me about himself.

"When your family found Hemlock Cove," he said, "they had trouble with… other forces at play. Evil forces. That's where my family came in. You see, Grace, although some call us warlocks, we're more like watchmen. Or to be politically correct, watch people."

"I don't understand," I said. "What is it you watch for, and how did you help my family? I wasn't told about any of this."

"That's because they didn't know." He smiled at me again and we came to a stop near the edge of the tide. The slow, lazy waves lapped at the sand, cooling our toes. The moon was bright and full in the sky, only occasionally obscured by a thin tendril of cloud.

"You'll have to explain more, Dario. I'm a facts kind of girl. Give me the nuts and bolts."

"That's what I like about you," he said, taking my hand and looking into my eyes.

I looked away and smiled. "Nope, you're not doing your weird woo-woo thing again until you tell me."

"We work in the shadows," he said finally. "Your kind and many others like you have faced persecution for many centuries, which is where my kind came in. We were very much like you. We had various abilities, but many suspicious groups and laypeople were scared of us, so we hid in the shadows and from then, over two thousand years ago, we vowed to protect others like us."

"So what did your family do for mine?"

"The same thing I did for you this morning," he said. "Though it goes in to more levels than that. Essentially, there are unseen entities that feed off witches' energy. They're unknown to you, like undetectable parasites. Many witches have been turned mad because of them. Think of them like energy leaches. I, and those that I come from, have the ability to combat these energy parasites."

"So you can see these things?" I asked as I looked over myself as though I had the sudden ability to spot these unseen things myself.

"Not directly," Dario said. "I'm not as powerful as my forebears—yet. I'm still young for one of my kind."

The waves were lapping deeper and covered my toes. I was so stunned I barely felt the cold water, yet my body, seemingly of its own volition, stepped back. Dario followed, and we were soon walking back across the beach toward the parking lot.

"So about this morning," I said as we walked. "You did

what exactly? Remove a parasite?"

"Something like that, yes. Your case wasn't as bad as some I have seen; I think you were a new target for these shadowy creatures. They were gathering around you, trying to understand how you work. They created a kind of dark aura around you; it's that which I noticed and decided to take evasive action on your behalf."

We stopped again and I turned to him. The moonlight reflected in various shades of silver off his smooth skin. He seemed to radiate light even without the moon's help. Why hadn't I noticed before that he was this… different, this special?

"Dario," I began, stepping closer so that our bodies almost touched, "thank you, thank you so much. I felt great when I arrived home, and it was as if a weight had been lifted, and for the first time in a long while I felt I could think straight."

"Ah, yes, the amulet," he said, staring down at me with those soulful eyes of his. "I heard that you pawned it. You know, if I had known the severity of your situation, I would have lent you the money. You only had to ask."

"You know I couldn't have done that," I said, grateful that he even thought of suggesting it. "I'm a proud woman. I've had to do things on my own for so long that I…"

"I understand," he said. "Samson was a good man. You two made a great team. For many years I was jealous of him, but I realized over the years that he complemented you so well that I couldn't help but be happy for you both."

We were getting in difficult territory. Although I had come to terms with my loss and realization that it was, eventually, okay to move on, talking about Samson so directly with Dario was too uncomfortable.

"To get back to these entity things," I said. "Where do they come from? And why were they sniffing around me? Are they also leeching energy from Joy and Hope?"

Dario placed a warm hand on my shoulder in reassurance. "They're both safe, I've made sure of that. And so are you, now. As to where they come from, that's still a great mystery. My family has spent many thousands of hours studying them and trying to source their origin, but we've never managed to do it; they're too ethereal to track down. We only see them when they already have started to manifest in our realm."

"Even though I felt good when I returned home," I said. "There's still something that's been bugging me. It's like there's something about this case that I should be able to see, some missing piece of the puzzle that's right there in plain view, but I just can't see through the fog. And also, why didn't you tell me what you wanted to do for me this morning?"

"It wouldn't have worked the same," he said. "If you knew what I was going to do, your subconscious would have been alerted to it, and so would the dark entities. I needed to surprise them, get in before they had a chance to really get their teeth into you."

"Well, thank you, you sweet, strange man."

"Strange?" He cocked an eyebrow and pulled an expression of mock surprise. "*Moi?*"

I gently nudged him with my elbow. "You're one of the strangest men I've ever met. But I like that… so think of it as a compliment."

We both stepped closer and slipped so easily into an embrace that it felt utterly natural. He was warm against me, and his delicate, sweet cologne tickled the edges of my nostrils. Our lips moved closer together and hung there for just a second, but it seemed like an eternity.

I kissed him then, delicate at first, and then more

passionately, my body melting into his as he pulled me close. We embraced and kissed, sweetly and gently. A light energy within me grew brighter and brighter until I felt as though I was floating.

My mind drifted away for a moment and I lost all sensation of body, and then right there, in that perfect moment, our energies intermingled in some inexplicable way and the thing that was bothering me about the case suddenly fell away and the truth shone like the sun.

I broke away from the kiss, sucked in a deep breath, and felt the weight of my body again as my soul, or whatever it was, came back to the physical world. Dario's eyes widened with slight alarm.

"What is it?" he said breathlessly.

"I know… I know who killed Greg Pelt! Quick, you drive while I call Zach. We need to go right now."

We rushed back to Dario's car, and while he drove to

my directions, I called Zach and got his voicemail again. I left him a message with all the details and hoped he would call me back before we arrived.

Chapter Fifteen

We got to Francesca's farmhouse in double quick time and parked a few hundred yards away so anyone inside wouldn't see us approach.

Although I had figured things out, I still didn't know who exactly was the killer. But I had narrowed it down—it was either Francesca or Abe.

Or possibly both, working as a team.

It was all to do with that blasted photo.

The answer was right there, staring us in the face all this time. But I'm jumping the gun; things weren't as cut and dry. I'll return to the photo shortly.

First, you need to know how it all went down at the farmhouse.

“We ought to wait until Zach arrives,” Dario said from the driver's seat.

My foot tapped nervously against the footrest as I watched the farmhouse. At first there were no lights on inside, but as we waited, I saw a light travel from one room to another. “I think someone's in there,” I said. “Looks like a candle.”

“You think their electricity is out?”

I shook my head. “Not likely. Francesca would have a generator. No, I think they're up to something no good. Do you detect anything emanating from there?”

“You mean the entities?”

"I do."

He stared out of the window for a few long seconds, concentration making his face stern. "I can't detect anything," he said.

"So that's good, right?"

"Not necessarily. It could mean that there's some dark magic going on there, creating a blanket to prevent scrying."

I reached for the door handle. "Only one thing for it, then," I said as I stepped out of the car and kicked off my heels.

"Grace," Dario whisper-shouted, even though we were in the middle of nowhere with the farmhouse a great distance from us. "What are you doing? We should wait for Zach."

"You're welcome to," I said. "But he might be hours; we don't know where he is or what he's doing. I want to nail the murderer as quick as I can before anything else bad happens. Trust me, this isn't my first rodeo."

Gently closing the door, I stepped carefully through the long grass and trees to get closer to the farmhouse.

Although I had done this many times before when serving with the police, I felt vulnerable without a firearm, my amulet, or Noah and Charity by my side. But it was clear to me something weird was going on in there, and I felt it was all tied to Greg Pelt's death.

I just needed evidence.

As I stalked closer to the barn, I regretted not stopping off to get a thicker coat.

My flimsy dress did nothing to stop the cold from freezing my skin. I didn't think it was natural, however, as it was far colder here than it was on the beach. The dark magic at work was my guess.

Dario wasn't too far behind me when I cast a look over

my shoulder. I signaled for him to stay back a few feet and follow me. We made our way slowly and quietly to the barn.

The main doors were open, mostly due to a lack of upkeep—the hinges had rusted off. They were wide enough for us to slip inside and snoop around. I expected to find Abe dozing in the hay, but he was nowhere to be seen.

Dario flicked on a narrow-beamed flashlight and from right beside me said, "What are we supposed to be looking for?"

"Shhhh!" I responded, putting my finger to my lips. I gestured for him to slowly arc the flashlight around the barn. The light picked out a number of rusted bits of machinery and some old oil drums.

I was going to suggest we move toward the house when something grabbed my attention. I took Dario's arm and moved it back in place. "There," I whispered in his ear. "Keep the light still." I then carefully stepped barefoot across the dusty floor to a pile of tools.

Wedged in the middle of the pile was a large wrench.

The image in my head that Hope had sent via Greg's spirit flashed brightly in recognition.

"What is it?" Dario asked as he stepped closer to me.

"The murder weapon," I said. "It confirms my suspicions. Someone in that house killed Greg Pelt. Don't touch it… it's better we leave it for Zach and the CSI guys. Come on, let's have a look around and see if we can see through a window or something."

"Grace, I really don't think this is a good idea. I'm getting a really bad vibe. Something's really not right here."

"Then it means we're on the right path," I said, adding a smile of reassurance, even though my own nerves felt strained.

I wasn't one to stop when I was on a roll, however.

With Zach or without him, I was onto something and I would finish it one way or another. Greg Pelt deserved that much at least. Besides, who knew how much time we had? I had learned early on in my career that you had to take an opportunity when it presented itself.

We left the barn and approached the house from the rear. An old dilapidated porch obscured any windows, meaning we had to creep closer. I picked up a shovel to use as a weapon if I needed to defend myself.

I noticed Dario hadn't armed himself, and as ever, he looked incredibly suave.

By the time we climbed up the wooden steps of the porch and approached the equally run-down door, we both heard the sound of movement on the other side. It was a muffled sound and a kind of murmuring, almost a chant.

"Stay here," Dario said quietly. "I'll take a closer look."

"Don't be daft, I used to be a cop," I said and pushed forward and tested the door handle carefully with a free hand, holding the shovel up with the other.

As soon as I turned it, the door swung open, knocking me to the side.

I dropped the shovel and grabbed hold of a porch upright to steady myself.

A large shadowy figure bundled out of the farm, a groaning noise coming from his throat.

"Abe?" I shouted as the light from inside the house spilled out, showing it was definitely him.

He looked completely out of it and somewhat drunk as he bundled forward and swung a meaty fist at Dario, who only just managed to block it, but the force of the blow knocked him back off the porch.

Abe turned his attention to me.

He lunged forward and I managed to duck under his wild swing, but when he spun round, he realized he had me cornered. I had nowhere else to go, trapped between the wall of the house and the balustrade of the porch.

"Abe, it's me, Grace," I shouted, attempting to get through to him, but his face just remained impassive.

He reached a powerful arm behind his back and pulled out a large wrench. The sight of it in his hands and the way he was stalking me sent a shiver down my spine.

I instinctively reached for my amulet in order to release its power in a desperate attempt to do anything and felt my bare neck.

The hulking figure lurched forward and swung the wrench. I tried to move free, but a shadow to my right bundled into me and then into Abe. Then a second shadow, much smaller this time, joined in the melee.

It was Noah and Charity!

Noah's momentum knocked the wrench from Abe's arm.

Charity launched up to his face and scratched at him with her claws, making him wheel backward in surprise and confusion. Dario appeared behind me and placed his hands on my shoulders. "Are you okay?" he asked.

"Yeah… just, you?"

There wasn't time for him to answer as he launched forward, his arms outstretched.

When he touched Abe's face, he uttered something in a guttural language I didn't understand and the larger man simply collapsed into a heap.

Noah and Charity jumped clear and sat beside Abe's still, prone body as though they were expecting him to reanimate at any moment.

And it didn't take long.

Within a few seconds, Abe started to groan again as he came round.

I peered through the door and noticed the candlelight increase. I was looking through the kitchen and into some kind of small reception room.

Fran was standing, cast in silhouette, leaning over some kind of urn with green smoke pouring from it.

She had her back to me and I took the opportunity to rush in, grabbing a rolling pin from the kitchen table along the way.

As soon as I stepped into the room, I knew what it was Francesca was using: a compulsion spell.

The urn was actually one of the jars that used to be in our kitchen.

The green smoke smelled of a mix of lavender and calamus root—a potent concoction designed to control another. It was pretty clear to me now that Abe was under such an influence.

I rushed in and smashed the urn with the rolling pin.

Francesca jumped back and slashed at me with a knife.

My heart rate leapt as I managed to lean away from the strike. Gripping the rolling pin, I lunged forward and rammed one end into Francesca's stomach.

She doubled over and dropped the knife just as Dario ran into the room and used his strange magic to subdue her like he had done with Abe.

I stamped on the still-burning root and herb mix to completely end the spell.

“What on earth is this?” Dario asked, scrunching his face up. “It stinks.”

“It's the key to this whole case,” I said. “Francesca's been using it to control Abe. Talking of which, where is he?”

“He's right here,” a new voice said. Zach!

My old friend was at the door with Abe in handcuffs. The big man looked like a zombie; his eyes were glossy and his face vacant. He was still coming down from the effects of Francesca's spell, and his lips moved without any words forming.

"I think you need to explain the situation," Zach said.

I helped Zach cuff both Francesca and Abe to chairs around the kitchen table. Dario stood guard at the door, and Noah and Charity milled about, their animal senses sending me all kinds of information. I was overwhelmed by the whole thing and couldn't really focus.

While Zach read Abe and Francesca their rights, I swept through the house, looking for more evidence. An urn of herbs wouldn't cut it in the courts; magic wasn't exactly taken into account these days.

I did, however, find an old lock and a set of lock picks in Francesca's bedroom. I recognized it immediately as a replica of the one we used to have on the rear door of the Cake & Bake. It was clear that Francesca had been the one to break in.

And given her abilities with the urn, it was clear we had another witch in town. Only someone with that kind of knowledge would have known what the components in our kitchen could be used for.

When I brought the lock down in a plastic bag, Francesca looked up at me with a scornful expression. Abe still looked confused and away with the fairies.

"You bitch!" Francesca said, spitting the words with bile.

I didn't rise to it. Instead, I revealed the evidence that had led me to her.

"You thought you were so clever with that photograph, didn't you?" I said. "Only when you changed the time on your cell phone to match that of your faulty clock, you forgot to switch off your TV."

"What are you talking about? You're mad!" Francesca said, struggling against the cuffs.

Zach and Dario looked at me with expectation, so I quickly got to the point.

I showed them the image and pointed to the small section of the TV screen in the corner.

"That show was broadcast live on air on the night of Greg's death," I said. "But the time it aired was later than what your clock and altered cell phone said it was. Which means it places you and Abe right in the window of the murder."

"That's ridiculous," she said. "No one's going to believe that. Have you never heard of Netflix?"

"But that show is a locally produced one that's not available on any on-demand service," I added. "And besides, I can prove the clock was faulty. When I questioned you, Noah picked up on an acidic scent that I recognized but couldn't quite place until earlier today."

"What was it?" Zach asked.

"Battery acid," I replied. "It was the same reason I was late for our lunch that time, and the same reason that TJ at the pawn shop today had problems with his computer mouse. We all bought batteries from the same faulty batch. That was why the clock stopped and gave Francesca here the brilliant idea of photographing an alibi."

The truth hit her hard and she slammed her knees against the kitchen table.

"Let me out of here!" she bellowed.

"Yeah, that's not going to happen," Zach said. "Remember the rights I read you? You should probably be quiet until you speak with a lawyer, for your sake—and Abe's. You're both already facing a murder charge."

"Screw the lawyers," she said, building up a froth of anger. "It's all over." She hung her head and looked over at the groggy figure of Abe. Her face softened and then the tears came, flowing down her cheeks and dripping onto the kitchen table.

We gave her a moment to compose herself.

"Are you all right?" Dario asked me, now standing right by my side.

"I am because of you," I said, squeezing his arm.

"It was all me," Francesca finally said. "Abe was innocent, even if he did deliver the fatal blow. I made him do it. He has no idea, no recollection."

Zach leaned forward and with a softer voice said, "You're going to have to explain all this back at the station. But we're going to have to take Abe with us too. We'll get it all squared out there, but ultimately, it'll be up to the DA's office. If you cooperate with us, it'll make things easier for Abe."

"Tell me one thing before you're taken away," I said to Francesca.

"What?"

"Why? Why have Abe kill Greg? What did he ever do to deserve that?"

She shrugged her shoulders and looked directly into my eyes. "Why does any woman kill a man?" She said nothing else, but I knew instantly what she meant.

She had loved Greg more than anything in the world, but he didn't love her back. He was a known cheat, perhaps never loved any woman in his life, especially the one who loved him more than anyone.

A couple of police cruisers pulled up outside, and Abe and Francesca were escorted away. Zach checked Dario and me to make sure we were okay, which we were, and then he headed off to follow up with all the paperwork and legal stuff.

"You did a great job today, Grace," Zach said. "I knew I could trust you to be the perfect partner. If you ever want your old job back…"

I shook my head and smiled. "No, thanks, I get enough excitement as a civilian. But I'm glad I could help."

Zach waved and left the house. The crime scene technicians escorted us out, as they wanted to scour the place for more evidence for the case. Dario took Noah, Charity, and me back to his car.

"Well, that was an unexpected first date," Dario said when we had all got safely inside and back on the road.

"I hope the next one will be a bit calmer," I added.

Noah was sitting on my lap, and Charity had managed to find a small space behind my seat. I could feel her emotions as she reconnected with me. She was still angry about the amulet business, but I felt her pride, and that eased a lot of my anxiety.

"So you want another date, then?" Dario asked.

"Of course, you owe Noah a doggy date, after all."

Noah's ears pricked up at that and he gave a cheerful woof before licking the side of my face. We spent the rest of the short journey back home in a comfortable, tired silence. I eased into the seat and fell into a nap as the rumble of the tires on the road lulled me to sleep… or was that Dario's efforts again?

Chapter Sixteen

You'll be pleased to know that we just managed to meet the deadline for the banquet.

When we got back home, Dario helped in the kitchen. It was actually great fun, as we all pitched in together… well, everyone except Hope, that is, but that was no surprise.

The next morning we all took the food up to the Ocean View event, and it went extremely well. We got a few requests for other events and our client paid us a bonus, which I placed down as a payment on the amulet, buying myself some extra time to raise the cash.

Kendra sadly had to return to Boston, but it was great to see her again, even if it was only for a short time.

On the upside, I had made plans with Dario for that doggy date in a few days' time. We had stayed in touch with nightly phone calls since 'the kiss', and I really felt like something good was going to develop there.

As far as Francesca and Abe went, the latter agreed to testify against Francesca and was thus given a deal. He'd still likely see jail time, but at a much reduced length given the level of manipulation displayed by Francesca, who had agreed to plead guilty.

A couple of days later I was sitting in the parlor with Joy and Nathaniel, enjoying some afternoon tea and pie. We were working out a new range of winter-themed products to help relaunch the Cake & Bake after all the recent controversy.

Noah, as ever, was loyal and by my side, probably making up for Charity's continuing chilliness towards me. But at least it wasn't open hostility. That was a good start.

I was just finishing up a slice of apple pie when the doorbell rang.

"I'll go," I said, patting my stomach. "I need to work off this cake baby."

"You're a darling," Joy said before reaching for another slice of pie.

I opened the door to find Michelle Dechamps standing there with a small box in her hands. At first I thought she had come to complain that I hadn't delivered any doggy bakes for her precious Fifi for the last few days.

I was about to go into it when she smiled and held up

a gloved hand.

She looked as stunning as ever, and she had a way of making me feel like a slob, especially as I still had pie crumbs on my flannel shirt.

"Please," Michelle said, "let me speak first, Grace. I know that you went to see David and that it came out that I had an accident and that I wasn't entirely honest with you about that."

"Or anyone else," I said. "Poor Casey. You could have seriously hurt her."

"I know, which is why I swerved out of the way. I knew what I was going to do was crazy, but I was… well, I can't explain it, I just had this moment of madness, as though I wasn't me. It was like something took over my mind that evening, and all I could see was rage because of Casey sleeping with Greg."

As she spoke, I pictured Francesca again, leaning over

the urn.

"Did you see Francesca before the whole Greg situation at all?" I asked.

"I did, yes. We had lunch together. I thought it was odd at the time when she called me. I only knew her by name and had seen her a few times in town, but we weren't friends, but there was just something about her that made me agree to see her. We had a nice lunch and spoke about Greg. I shared my disappointment about his cheating with her."

"And how soon after that did you decide it would be a great idea to run over Casey in your lovely new car?"

"Well, it was later that same day. What are you saying, Grace?"

"Oh, nothing, it's just weird to me how things get jumbled up together. It's a small town, after all, so I suppose these connections are going to happen."

I smiled at her to let her know it was nothing, but it was quite clear to me now that Michelle was another victim of Francesca's dark magic and dark intensions. It made me wonder just how far her meddling went.

"Oh, okay," Michelle said and then, seemingly remembering why she had come, added, "Because of you, I managed to clear my conscience. I hated what I was going to do, and I spoke with Zachary and the police, admitting that I had driven dangerously. I've had my license suspended for twelve months, but I'm so glad to have that weight off my shoulders. I'm not good with all that kind of thing."

"Um, it was my pleasure?" I said, not really sure what else to say. I was just doing my job with questioning David, and I couldn't keep her actions a secret. But I was happy for her that she could feel good about herself for confessing, even if the truth was that it was entirely down to her, but I couldn't start explaining that to her. She'd think I was mad… well, more mad than most people thought I already was.

"So, I bought you a gift to say thank you," Michelle said, handing me the small box.

I opened it and gasped.

It was the amulet.

"Michelle! This is… amazing, but it was so expensive, how could I ever thank you? I don't think you could ever know how much this means to me."

Michelle beamed a wide smile at seeing my happiness. "Of course I know," she said. "I've never seen you without it, and when I saw it there in Patty's, I knew something terrible must have happened for you to have given it up. But as for the cost, don't worry about it, I honestly can't tell you how much better I feel for the truth coming out, but I do want to ask for a small favor in return."

"Anything," I said, wiping a tear from my eye before

placing the amulet around my neck. My skin buzzed as soon as it touched me. I felt whole again and re-energized. "Please, just name it."

I was expecting her to ask me to be a housemaid or something, but she simply said, "Double amount of doggy bakes for Fifi for the next month and we're quits."

"Is that all?" I asked. "I owe you so much more than that."

"Those are my terms, Grace, and I'm in no mood for negotiation. Besides, I'm busy and it looks like you've got a guest. I'll see you first thing tomorrow morning with Fifi's treats."

She whirled away on her expensive heels and raised a gloved hand to me as she got into the back of a long black car. Behind her ride was a familiar car: a classic Maserati.

Dario had come to visit. My day really couldn't have

got any better!

But it did.

Later, while we were all relaxing in the parlor, watching a Hercule Poirot film—*Death on the Nile* as it happens—Charity jumped up onto my lap and pawed gently at the amulet. Her eyes locked onto mine and I felt a wave of both relieve and love from her.

I gave her cheeks a little rub and then she curled up on my lap, purring contently. Noah was asleep beneath my legs and Dario was sitting next to me, his arm over my shoulder. For the first time in ages, I felt utterly content and massively satisfied that we had brought Greg Pelt's killer to justice.

But I wouldn't remain relaxed and content for too long.

Hemlock Cove would soon experience another strange case that would stretch all my skills to the limits, and even with the help of Noah, Charity, and Dario, I would face the biggest challenge of my life so far. But that's a story for another time. I hope to be able to tell it to you soon. Take care, and watch out for dark magic!

Click here to learn what happens in book 2!

(Or type this into your web browser: http://kennedychasebooks.com/amm)

Author's Note

Thank you so much for reading my novel; it means a great deal to me to know people are enjoying my books. If you liked the book, may I kindly ask you to leave a review.

As a small publisher I have to do all the marketing and promotion for my books and you can really help out an independent author by letting other readers know you enjoyed the book. Even a couple of sentences would be hugely appreciated.

If you would like to know more about my books and be alerted to new releases, you can sign-up to my strictly no-spam email list here or by navigating to: http://bit.ly/kchase with your web browser.

I only send updates of new releases or special offers. Thank you again for your support and I hope to send you news of exciting new titles very soon!

Sign-up to the Mystery Parlor mailing list.

(Or type this into your browser: http://bit.ly/kchase)

Books by Kennedy Chase

Witches of Hemlock Cove

A Mystic Murder

A Cryptic Case - Early 2016

Harley Hill Mysteries

Murder on the Hill

Murder on the Page

Murder in the Kitchen

Murder in the Cake

Made in the USA
Middletown, DE
24 February 2017